# STAR WARS

# WOMEN OF THE GALAXY

# STAR WARS

# WOMEN OF THE GALAXY

BY AMY RATCLIFFE • FOREWORD BY KATHLEEN KENNEDY

CHRONICLE BOOKS
SAN FRANCISCO

Library of Congress Cataloging-in-Publication Data available.

ISBN 978-1-4521-6631-5

Manufactured in China

Jacket and case illustrations by **Jen Bartel**
Jacket and case design by **Michael Morris**
Interior design by **Jenna Huerta**
Lucasfilm Publishing Creative Director, **Michael Siglain**
Lucasfilm Art Director, **Troy Alders**

10 9 8 7 6 5 4 3 2 1

Chronicle Books LLC
680 Second Street
San Francisco, CA 94107
www.chroniclebooks.com

© & TM 2018 LUCASFILM

www.starwars.com

*For Carrie Fisher*

# Contents

# Foreword

I was in the early stages of my career as a filmmaker when *Star Wars* came out in 1977. With that first film, and the cultural phenomenon that followed, George Lucas introduced the world to Princess Leia, a character who stood apart from most female leads of the day. With strength, courage, a quick wit and grit, she could easily hold her own against the predominantly male cast, including Darth Vader himself. I was immediately struck by the possibilities of this universe George created—boundless storytelling potential combined with a rare opportunity to explore universal themes that have endured through the ages. I was captivated.

In the decades since, George and others have fleshed out the *Star Wars* universe with hundreds of new characters, including the heroes, villains, rebels, and rogues highlighted in this book. While not all of these characters are cut out to be heroes like Padmé, Rey, and Ahsoka, it's important that they occupy a wide range of roles in the *Star Wars* galaxy, and act capably, skillfully, and formidably within them.

In *Star Wars*, we are fortunate to have such a broad platform from which to tell our stories. In addition to the films, there are animated series, novels, comics, games, and more, all allowing us to further explore this rich galaxy and the many characters in it. It's a testament to George's vision that what he began as a story to inspire, we continue to embrace as a beacon of empowerment and hope.

Kathleen Kennedy

# Introduction

The characters in this book make the *Star Wars* we know possible. They are heroes and villains, Sith and Jedi, senators and scoundrels, mothers, mercenaries, artists, pilots—anything and everything—and their stories drive the galaxy forward in epic, but also important if less flashy ways. The Rebel Alliance wouldn't exist without Mon Mothma. The New Republic wouldn't discover the Empire's remnants on Jakku without Norra Wexley. Invaluable information from the Jedi Archives would be lost if not preserved by lightsaber-wielding librarian Jocasta Nu. Their stories extend across the films, animated series, novels, comics, and games, often crossing over to continue from one medium (for instance, we can follow Leia Organa's adventures through them all). And there's a galaxy of fascinating characters to discover beyond the film trilogies. In the *Aftermath* novels, we can marvel as Kyrsta Agate takes down a Super Star Destroyer using a tractor beam. In *The Clone Wars* and *Star Wars Rebels*, we meet one of the most important heroes in the *Star Wars* saga, Ahsoka Tano.

Ahsoka has had a profound impact upon me. In some ways, I grew into *Star Wars* fandom through her. I first saw the films as a teenager, but I didn't find my *Star Wars* until *The Clone Wars*—in no small part due to discovering Ahsoka. Seeing her as a young Padawan alongside Anakin Skywalker, one of the heroes of the *Star Wars* galaxy, acting snippy and a little immature, but also confident and capable, grabbed my attention. I was fascinated to watch her navigate her way through lessons from her atypical Jedi Master, make mistakes, and adapt. I was blown away when she decided to leave the Jedi Order, the only life she'd ever known. Her actions gave me courage. And the inclusion of a female teenage lead made me feel positive about the future of *Star Wars*.

In passionately fangirling about Ahsoka and *The Clone Wars* on social media and my blog, I found my passion: writing. Ahsoka's determination inspired me to work toward a dream. As I discovered my voice and pursued my own goals, she was maturing and questioning the world around her. By the time she returned in *Star Wars Rebels*, older and wiser, I felt that I was, too. And I continue to learn from her.

I connect with Ahsoka the most, but she is far from the only *Star Wars* character who moves me. When I need courage, I'm bolstered by Leia's no-nonsense attitude and optimism. When I need to speak so people will listen, I'm energized by Padmé's intelligence and commanding presence. When I need to find light in a dark situation, I'm encouraged by Rey's unflinching kindness and deep strength.

With *Women of the Galaxy*, I want to highlight the accomplishments of female characters in *Star Wars*. I want to share the actions that make me hold a character in awe and excitedly text a friend, "Can you believe she did that?" but also to talk about the quieter moments that help us relate to them. I want to emphasize how everyone makes a difference, whether she's an Imperial officer, a Rebel hero, a diplomat, or a mother. We are all part of the story, and we all deserve to have our story told.

Fictional characters have the power to influence us, to push us into action, to give us constants in a world full of variables. It's why stories are never *just* stories. I hope you will find inspiration in these characters and in this book.

# Aayla Secura

*"Isn't liberty worth fighting for?"*

ᚲᚲᚡᛃᚲ ᛃᚢᛗᚺᛒ7ᚲ

Imagine being a production assistant at Lucasfilm's special effects company, Industrial Light & Magic, getting the chance to work on a stage unit for *Attack of the Clones*, and then being asked to be in the film. Amy Allen lived this extraordinary turn of events and played the Twi'lek Jedi Master Aayla Secura in *Attack of the Clones* and *Revenge of the Sith*. Inspired by seeing Aayla on a comic book cover, George Lucas added the fan-favorite well into post-production of *Clones* (costume supervisor Gillian Libbert had only two weeks to design Aayla's costume for Lucas's approval), and so the blue-skinned Jedi makes a grand entrance swinging a lightsaber in the Battle of Geonosis. Since Twi'leks hadn't been featured in an action heavy role previous to the film, she struck a chord, inspiring fans to craft the species' distinctive lekku head tentacles and paint their skin for Aayla costumes.

Aayla's story continues in animated form in *Star Wars: The Clone Wars*. As a Jedi General in the conflict, she leads charges around the galaxy, fights to protect planets from Separatist invasion, and works with fellow Jedi Obi-Wan Kenobi, Mace Windu, and Tiplee to investigate Darth Maul's activities. She also takes point at the Battle of Quell, guiding Ahsoka Tano and the clone troopers through a crash, before which she uses the Force to turn their cruiser's power back on, and a surprise attack on the planet Maridun. She's a tal-

"A strong belief can be more powerful than any army."
—Aayla Secura

ented and athletic fighter, eschewing Jedi robes for a greater range of movement—a freedom evident as she leaps along the back of the gargantuan Zillo Beast as it crushes its way through Coruscant. And she's wise, advising Ahsoka not to let her personal affection for her Master, Anakin Skywalker, cloud her ability to make necessary, hard decisions in battle. Aayla recognizes the danger of attachment, having overcome a similar struggle with her own teacher, Quinlan Vos, who she saw as a father figure. "I realized that for the greater good, I had to let him go," she tells Ahsoka, "Don't lose a thousand lives just to save one."

Aayla is a playable character in 2005's *Star Wars: Battlefront II* game, which is an easier way of embodying the character than Allen's four-hour makeup process in portraying her on film, though she's delighted to have had the experience. "The popularity of the character is overwhelming and truly special. I am not really sure how to explain it. I just feel so fortunate to be a part of Star Wars. It's part of history."

# Adi Gallia

A Jedi Council member ready to take the fight to the Separatists.

ᕽᔿ1 ᗡᕽ ᒎᒎ1ᕽ

Force-sensitive children come to the Jedi from all walks of life. Adi Gallia, introduced in *The Phantom Menace*, is born to diplomats on Coruscant (the distinctive headdress she wears is a tribute to her Tholothian heritage), and the Jedi Order perceived Adi's connection to the Force and brought her to the Jedi Temple. An astute observer, she raises suspicion about the Trade Federation's enterprises in the Naboo system during her time serving on the Jedi Council. Investigation of the Federation's blockade of Naboo brings Queen Amidala into the *Star Wars* galaxy and makes the Council aware of the increasing Separatist threat.

Adi's also unafraid of a fight, balancing her use of the Force and what it means to be a Jedi with an aggression toward Separatist enemies. Throughout her appearances in *Star Wars: The Clone Wars*, she puts herself in the middle of the action, whether it's developing a high-risk but successful plan to rescue Jedi Master Eeth Koth from General Grievous's metal clutches, evading Grievous herself, or helping Obi-Wan search for Darth Maul and Savage Opress in the Outer Rim.

# Ahsoka Tano

*"This is a new day, a new beginning."*

ᚲᛖᚢᛟᛃᚲ ᛃᚲᚾᚨ

The Clone Wars animated film debut in 2008 brought an unforgettable new character to the *Star Wars* saga. Ahsoka Tano, appointed by Yoda to be Anakin Skywalker's Padawan learner, is the first female Jedi lead introduced to the saga on-screen. She's a character a generation of fans has grown up watching, as she herself has grown. The Togruta is fourteen years old when we first meet her, and we watch her transform from "Snips," a nickname Anakin gives her for being snippy, to a Jedi hero of the Clone Wars, to the Rebel agent Fulcrum, to a wise mentor. It's the sort of arc that we have the chance to follow for relatively few characters in *Star Wars*, and it gives us the chance to really connect with Ahsoka as we accompany her on her journey.

And it was always meant to be *her* journey. When George Lucas first envisioned the idea of Anakin having a Padawan between *Attack of the Clones* and *Revenge of the Sith*, he wanted the Jedi-in-training to be a girl. We meet Ahsoka as a learner, but she's already holding her own in wit and battle against the more experienced Anakin and Obi-Wan Kenobi. She even gives Anakin his own nickname, "SkyGuy." Ahsoka brings a fresh perspective, questioning why things are the way they are. And she doesn't always heed Anakin's advice, giving Anakin a taste of what Obi-Wan must have felt teaching him, too.

Ahsoka's ask-questions-and-take-action spirit also galvanized voice actress Ashley Eckstein. When attending conventions and events for her part in portraying Ahsoka in the film, Eckstein observed both the large number of female *Star Wars* fans and the dearth of female-focused merchandise. To help foster this growing audience, Eckstein founded Her Universe, an apparel company that began with selling *Star Wars* T-shirts in women's sizes and cuts, and which has since expanded to make female fans across fandoms feel included.

Ahsoka's story begins when Jedi master Plo Koon discovers her and her Force talents when she's only three years old. She's raised in the Jedi Temple on Coruscant, and she trains in a tumultuous time. By the time she's a Padawan, the Clone Wars have begun. Her introduction to her master, Anakin, happens in the midst of battle, and Ahsoka must then and there learn to balance a Jedi's role as a guardian of peace, who isn't supposed to attack, while leading clone troopers into combat. It's a paradox, but she manages. Later skirmishes against Separatist forces help teach Ahsoka to strategize and command, but in learning we also see her make tragic mistakes, such as losing an entire squadron of pilots after disobeying orders in the Battle of Ryloth.

Ahsoka observes Anakin's courage and occasional recklessness and is more willing to take risks because of it, and as she trains with him, she forms a close bond with her teacher. She also finds Anakin's lax attitude and unconventional methods an invitation for a little sass, unafraid to knock him down a peg with lines like, "Master, if you have taught me one thing, it's that nothing is easy when you are around." The true depth of their connection is evident when Ahsoka is twisted against Anakin by the dark side while on the planet Mortis. She dies, and Anakin becomes the conduit for the healing life force that brings Ahsoka back. He would do anything for her.

The independence that Anakin helps Ahsoka find in herself is crucial to her character. After she's betrayed by her friend Barriss Offee and framed for bombing the Jedi Temple, she's expelled by the Jedi Order despite her plea of innocence, and

given to the Republic for trial. The truth prevails, and though the Jedi Council welcomes her back, characterizing the events as a test, she decides that she must make her own way. She tells Anakin, "I can't stay here any longer, not now. I have to sort this out on my own, without the Council and without you."

It's a pivotal moment. Ahsoka has spent most of her life within the Jedi Order. Her belief system, her identity, almost everything she knows is interwoven with the Jedi creed. That she is willing to step away so decisively when she loses faith is an act of enormous bravery, and another measure of her growing maturity through hard-earned wisdom.

In the novel *Ahsoka*, we follow her path after the near-annihilation of the Jedi in the execution of the evil Darth Sidious's deadly Order 66. She doesn't go into hiding, like some surviving Jedi. She forges her lightsabers, the first white blades in the *Star Wars* saga, and she fights. Her actions on the Outer Rim moon Raada—sowing the seeds of discord among the locals after the Empire arrives—attract the attention of Bail Organa, who recruits her for the Rebellion. She's unwilling to take part in the war as a commander or officer, but she agrees to help disseminate classified information to Rebel cells as an operative codenamed Fulcrum.

It's in this role that Ahsoka encounters the crew of the *Ghost*, reentering the animated galaxy in *Star Wars Rebels*. Fans exhilarated by the return of the beloved character celebrated by flooding social media with the hashtag #AhsokaLives. Eckstein was also thrilled to be back, and to explore a new, more mature side of Ahsoka. "She's now back with a sense of confidence. We could all take that with us—to approach whatever we do with a strong sense of confidence, to speak with authority, to feel comfortable with what we know and putting that into action," she observes. "It's almost like when we go to school for so many years and then when we graduate, we're out in the real world. It's like Ahsoka is now out in the real world, and we now see her in her job and she is very confident."

She becomes a supporting adviser of sorts for the Rebel cell Phoenix Squadron, occasionally accompanying Ezra Bridger and his Jedi mentor Kanan Jarrus on missions. During one of these excursions, she encounters Darth Vader, and finally learns the devastating truth about Anakin's transformation and turn to the dark side. Ahsoka feels partly responsible for his downfall, having left years earlier, and confronts her conscience when his helmet is slashed in an epic battle, revealing Anakin's face beneath Vader's mask. She vows not to leave him again, but it's too late. Her flashing white sabers allow Ezra to escape, and he is in turn later able to save her by pulling her through a portal from the future. Kanan has since been killed in battle, and Ahsoka offers Ezra the devastating realization, "You can't save your master, and I can't save mine." Before Ahsoka returns safely to her own time, to continue her journey through the past, Ezra tells her to come find him when she gets back. She fulfills that promise when she appears on Lothal five years later, an enigmatic figure of mystical wisdom, to help Sabine search for Ezra. Her journey continues.

*"To defeat your enemy, you
have to understand them."*

**—Ahsoka Tano**

# Amilyn Holdo

*"In every corner of the galaxy, the downtrodden and oppressed know our symbol and they put their hope in it. We are the spark that will light the fire."*

⨯⟋⊣⋁⋏ ⩛⧠⟍⟋⟁

The Resistance is even more ragtag than the Rebel Alliance, thin on resources, and often making do with rickety equipment from the Galactic Civil War era. So when the first photos from *The Last Jedi* showed Vice Admiral Amilyn Holdo with her coiffed purple hair, elegant mauve dress, and striking silver accessories in the midst of the drab browns and grubby oranges of the Resistance surroundings, they caused ripples through fandom. Who was this woman? Was she an aristocrat? Was she a politician who survived the fall of the New Republic?

*Leia, Princess of Alderaan* introduces us to a young Amilyn, who, like Leia Organa and other politically-minded teenagers, joins the Apprentice Legislature of the Imperial Senate. After introducing herself to Leia in a pathfinding class (a course teaching outdoor basics, especially how to navigate without the assistance of tools), her first words are: "I hope it's dangerous. I want to get more comfortable with the nearness and inevitability of death." Candid, and unexpectedly unlike other aspiring politicians and diplomats, Amilyn establishes being different and accepts it as a cornerstone of her personality. It's refreshing to see someone so at home in her own skin. And, being who she is, Amilyn thinks everyone is special, too. She tells a fellow apprentice legislator, "Rarity is an illusion, because every person and object in the galaxy is in some way unique."

# "Godspeed, Rebels"

## —Amilyn Holdo

Claudia Gray, author of *Princess of Alderaan*, was pleased to see fans' positive reactions to Amilyn: "She's somebody who's a bit off-kilter, who sees the world through a prism most others don't understand. At first Leia thinks she's pleasant but weird, but as time goes on, it becomes apparent there's much more to Holdo than you might guess when you first meet her. We don't really have a lot of true oddballs in *Star Wars*, so it was fun to introduce one."

While her native world of Gatalenta is known for its independent spirit and tranquility, Amilyn is more assertive. She displays her individualism by frequently changing her hair color and donning outfits with vivid hues and patterns in contrast to more common, neutral tones. Instead of meditating, she throws herself into adventures. When Leia starts learning more about the dangers of the Empire, Amilyn stows away with her in an Imperial informant's ship to gain intelligence about his activities.

By the time we see her again in *The Last Jedi*, some thirty-five years later, Amilyn has matured, and so has her friendship with Leia. She's been part of the Rebellion, and now, the Resistance. When the First Order delivers a blow that wipes out most of the Resistance's officers and injures Leia, Amilyn steps in to command the beleaguered *Raddus*. She projects confidence when she gathers the remaining forces and tells them, "We are the spark that will light the fire that will restore the Republic."

Since the First Order is tracking the Resistance through hyperspace and chances of an escape by that means are slim, she stays the course, keeping the *Raddus* out of the reach of First Order cannons. Her steely shutdown of Poe Dameron's hot-take impulse to recklessly fight back illustrates the difference between being a leader and being a hero. Her singular responsibility is keeping as much of the Resistance alive as possible, which she does by ordering full evacuation via transport ships while she remains aboard the *Raddus*. When the First Order turns their lasers upon the transports, Amilyn's clear-eyed strength comes into focus. By taking the *Raddus* into hyperspace right through the enemy ships, she gives the Resistance the chance to get to the surface of the shadow planet of Crait, to continue the fight. The spark does not go out.

# Arihnda Pryce

*"I serve the Empire until the end."*

KꓶIƎ∧ꓶK ᑌ�时Ꝟ𝟦ⵠ

You don't want to cross Arihnda Pryce. Ambitious, ruthless, and willing to step on anyone who gets in the way as she climbs to power, she's a model Imperial officer. Born on the planet Lothal and perhaps destined to go into the family mining business, from childhood Arihnda dreams of something bigger and brighter. She eventually seizes upon the opportunity to get offworld by working for one of Lothal's senators on Coruscant. From there she leverages connections, and when she can, gathers dirt on Imperial officers—because you never know what will come in handy. Her strategy works, and when we first officially meet her in *Star Wars Rebels*, she's the governor of Lothal.

Voice actress Mary Elizabeth McGlynn thinks Arihnda is, well, kind of despicable, but she applauds her persistence, and she has fun playing a driven character whose accomplishments are never quite enough. "There's something fascinating about giving voice to a woman who is so desperate for power and yet seemingly so ineffective at achieving her goals," McGlynn says. "She wants to capture or kill the Rebels. She can't. She thinks she can control Imperial Grand Admiral Thrawn. She can't. So her frustration continues to grow as the plot unfolds. That only adds to her desperation to complete her goal, at any cost."

Arihnda is shrewd. She uses data about a group of Rebels to convince Grand Moff Tarkin to give her the governorship. And she's observant. She notes Thrawn as an up-and-comer before his many promotions, and when she understands he could use help navigating the Imperial bureaucracy, she's happy to lend a hand. For a price.

# Asajj Ventress

*"It's only the likes of me, with nothing to lose, who'll really be prepared to tear the galaxy down and start over."*

ᚴᚾᚴᚵᚵ ᚧᚹᚾᚵᚹᚾᚵᚾ

Asajj Ventress kills a male bounty hunter who pesters her in Mos Eisley's cantina and calls her a "pretty bald babe." A Dathomirian Force-user who first brandishes her dual red lightsabers in *Star Wars: The Clone Wars*, Asajj has been an assassin, a Nightsister, and a bounty hunter—sometimes all at once. How she gets by is fluid, but a constant current is her driving anger and thirst for revenge.

Her history is one of abandonment. The Nightsister clan, her family, is forced to give her up when she's an infant. The pirate who takes her from Dathomir is killed. The Jedi Master who finds her after she's orphaned and trains her as his Padawan is shot. In despair and rage, Asajj turns to the dark side. She uses bitterness and a desire for vengeance against anyone who wrongs her. Anger gives her strength, and the Separatist leader Count Dooku takes notice.

He takes Asajj on as his personal assassin and, as a tool and weapon of the Separatists, Asajj relishes tormenting citizens and Jedi alike. She's a menacing figure who wields her lightsabers and moves with terrifying speed. Frequently tangling with Anakin Skywalker and Obi-Wan Kenobi, she never quite defeats them, but they are well-matched (in one battle, we see her Force-choke both Jedi at once).

Though Asajj devotes her service to Dooku, the Count is loyal to Darth Sidious, who sees a threat in Asajj's growing power and orders her killed. She survives, but is again alone.

The idea of delving into the details of Asajj's past came from George Lucas. Her backstory was previously explored for other stories, and in fact, the character's look sprung from unused concept art by Dermot Power for *Attack of the Clones*. That art found purpose in the "Nightsisters" arc of *The Clone Wars*; Lucas wanted to show the narrative from her point of view and expand her story. Voice actress Nika Futterman said one of the biggest mysteries of portraying Asajj was figuring out who she was, as Futterman knew just as much or as little as the audience: "I just assumed she had a difficult childhood!" Careful not to play her as a one-note character, she left room to adjust once Asajj's backstory was revealed.

To start over, Asajj returns home. Mother Talzin, leader of the Nightsisters, welcomes her. The reunion showcases the tight-knit nature of the sisterhood, as Asajj's fellow clan members are willing to aid her in her quest for retribution against Dooku. She pours all her intensity into killing the Sith Lord, first trying to murder him herself, and then working with Mother Talzin to train the Nightbrother Savage Opress to handle the deed. But Dooku turns the tables and brings death to Dathomir, wiping out the Nightsisters.

Asajj moves on once again, this time with the added burden of guilt. The massacre leaves her deeply shaken, but now more open to the light. She lends assistance to Ahsoka Tano, who once used to call Asajj the "Hairless Harpy," when the Togruta rebel is on the run after being framed for a crime. She hasn't fallen so far astray that she can't put herself in Ahsoka's place.

Asajj's trajectory continues in author Christie Golden's novel *Dark Disciple*, adapted from elements of unproduced scripts after the end of *The Clone Wars* series. In the novel, through a begrudging partnership with the Jedi Quinlan Vos, Asajj understands the futility of vengeance and reconnects with estranged emotions of compassion and forgiveness. Sacrificing herself to save Quinlan, she says, "You always have a choice to be better. You always have a choice to pick the right path. Even if that choice comes a little late."

"You always have a choice to be better. You always have a choice to pick the right path."

—Asajj Ventress

# Aunt Z

An enterprising and brazen tavern owner on the Colossus.

ᴋᴏᴧ↓ ᴅ

Racing is a profitable sport, and Aunt Z'Vk'Thkrkza, called Aunt Z for short, knows how to leverage the competitions on the Colossus platform to her advantage without jumping into the pilot's seat. Introduced in *Star Wars Resistance*, the grumpy, snarky Gilliand has a sharp mind for business, and her namesake Aunt Z's Tavern is the most popular eatery and bar on the Colossus. It's known as *the* hangout for the platform's star pilots, the Aces, as well as a gathering place for usual bar-dwellers and travelers passing through. Everyone's welcome as long as they leave generous tips and don't act up.

While her assistant bartender—the multi-limbed service droid G1-7CH (aka "Glitch")—slings drinks, Aunt Z doles out insightful and blunt advice. Platform denizens go to her for answers, and she provides guidance depending on how much she favors who is asking, and how much they are tipping. But patrons shouldn't expect Aunt Z to coddle them, despite her cozy nickname. She's all about making a profit, and employs an imposing Klatooinian enforcer, Bolza Grool, to ensure customers stay in line and don't skip out on their bills.

# Aurra Sing

*"I never ask for permission to do anything."*

ᚲᛃᚱᚱᚲ ᛋᛁᛀᚷ

First spotted in the stands watching the Boonta Eve Classic podrace in *The Phantom Menace*, we don't observe Aurra's lethal talents until *Star Wars: The Clone Wars*, when she joins a young Boba Fett in his vengeful pursuit of Jedi Master Mace Windu. A bounty hunter and one of the deadliest assassins in the galaxy, she specializes in sniper attacks with her projectile rifle, but she has no problem handling herself in close combat with other weaponry, such as the lightsabers she's kept as trophies from the Jedi she's hunted. The biocomputer implanted in her skull also helps give her an edge.

Aurra's interests and motivations are always her own. It's certainly not kindness that leads her to take future bounty hunter Boba Fett under her wing after Windu murders his father, Jango. She works with Boba as part of her crew, ruthlessly stokes his need for payback, and coolly abandons him after he's captured, teaching him a valuable moral lesson: trust no one. Aurra also shows Boba how to take advantage of relationships. Her former flame, the ebullient and connected pirate Hondo Ohnaka, means nothing more to her than a place to hide from Jedi.

Jaime King voices Aurra in *The Clone Wars*, and empathizes with the character at a certain level. "She's hardcore, and that's why it's so fun to play her, because it's not anything you could ever get away with in real life. When you're acting, then you can get away with it through your characters, so it's like you get to express these sides of yourself that you never do. What's really exciting is just learning about Aurra, learning about her life and learning about what she's up to and how she manipulates to get what she wants."

# Barriss Offee

*"I've come to realize what many people in the Republic have come to realize: that the Jedi are the ones responsible for this war."*

ꓱꓗꓷꓳꓲꓠꓥꓠ ꓳꓭꓸꓺꓦꓲꓦꓲ

Disillusionment can lead to drastic measures. In *Attack of the Clones* and the beginning of *Star Wars: The Clone Wars,* we meet Offee as Padawan to Jedi Master and fellow Mirialan, Luminara Unduli. Barriss is studious, well-mannered, and respectful (in many ways the opposite of her friend Ahsoka Tano.) She's the very picture of an exemplary Jedi apprentice, until she orchestrates the bombing of the Jedi Temple on Coruscant.

Barriss comes to believe the Jedi are responsible for the Clone Wars and meets with a Coruscanti woman, Letta Turmond, who agrees; they plan the attack on the Temple together to make a statement. She frames Ahsoka for the bombing and for the murder of Letta (Barriss killed her to keep her quiet). Afterwards, Barriss tells the court, "We've so lost our way that we have become villains in this conflict." While her beliefs might not be wrong, Barriss is imprisoned for her actions. As Ahsoka observes: "She had a point about the Republic and the Jedi. There was something wrong with them, and we were too locked into our traditions to see what it was."

# Bazine Netal

*"People will believe what I want them to believe.
They always do."*

Ǝ⋉ᗡ1ᐱⅤ ∧Ⅴ1ᒍ⋉ᒍ

Bounty hunters are often specialists: they excel at slicing and manipulating data, or thievery, or assassination, or killing in their own special way. But Bazine Netal can do it all, hacking, stealing, and murdering with her choice of snub-nosed blaster, poisoned dagger, or throwing knives. Taken from an orphanage on the desert planet Chaaktil when she was a child, she endured brutal lessons. Her captor, Delphi Kloda, adopted her with the purpose of training her in his combat school and turning her into a perfect weapon that would be his to wield. She left her past behind and adopted the pseudonym Bazine. As she says about her time there, "My friends were grizzled murderers who taught me how to punch."

Bazine combines her cunning with ingenuity. For example, the outfit she wears in *The Force Awakens* when she alerts the First Order to BB-8's location, at Maz Kanata's castle in Takodana, is more than a striking fashion choice. The baffleweave dress jams sensors, her boot wedges conceal thermal detonators, and the black Rishi eel ink on her fingers obscures her fingerprints. A master of disguise, Bazine keeps her secrets close.

In the *Flight of the Falcon* storyline across books and comics, Bazine travels to the distant planet of Batuu at the edge of the galaxy while on the hunt for the *Millennium Falcon*. Sifting truth from tall tales, she pursues the legendary freighter that Imperials and bounty hunters alike have almost, but never quite, snared.

# Beru Lars

A talented cook, a savvy moisture farmer, and the woman who raised Luke Skywalker.

ᗕᐯᓮᒲ ᒍᗏᒿ7ᔑ

*Star Wars* is a galaxy full of heroes and villains, daring pilots, and fearless warriors. Of course, they get most of the attention, but it takes all kinds of characters to keep the story moving. Beru Whitesun Lars is first introduced to fans as Aunt Beru, a.k.a. the woman pouring the blue milk in *A New Hope.* But as the adoptive mother of Luke Skywalker, she helps raise the farm boy turned hero for nineteen years, supporting his hopes and dreams, and particularly advocating that he be allowed to attend the Imperial Academy rather than spend endless seasons on the Lars' moisture farm.

Beru also has dreams of her own. Her cooking class teacher compliments her work (a blue-milk cheese), saying it's the best he's ever tasted, and she strongly considers opening a café of her own in nearby Anchorhead. Before adopting Luke, she and her husband Owen want to have children of their own, but with the arrival of young Skywalker, she becomes dedicated to their new family and keeping Luke safe from the perils of Tatooine, and his true father, Anakin Skywalker / Darth Vader. She observes, "I was born to make people feel good when everything around them seemed just awful."

Because Beru appears in the original trilogy and the prequel trilogy set some nineteen years earlier, she's portrayed on film by two actresses, first in 1977 by Shelagh Fraser, and then by Bonnie Piesse. When she was cast for *Attack of the Clones*, Piesse watched *A New Hope* to study Fraser's accent and physical mannerisms, as well as what Beru would have been like earlier in her life. "I watched the scenes with Beru from *A New Hope* over and over until I felt I had a good sense of the character's nature. She seemed very kind, grounded, and loving to me, so that's what I tried to bring to the role. I also felt that, as I was playing her when she's younger, I wanted to bring in a little shyness."

# Bo-Katan Kryze

*"Mandalore will survive. We always survive."*

ᔐᕟ˙ᘃᛕ⳨ᛕᗺ ᘃ⍑ᐁᗺ

Bo-Katan Kryze is a warrior of deep conviction. Born on the planet Mandalore to Clan Kryze and first seen in *Star Wars: The Clone Wars*, she's committed to the traditions of Mandalore's martial past. When her sister Satine Kryze, the Duchess of Mandalore, puts a pacifistic system in place following the end of the planet's latest civil war, Bo-Katan immediately joins Death Watch, a terrorist group opposed to Mandalore's government and its shift in direction. Bo-Katan loves her sister, but her drive to preserve the fierce heritage of their world is powerful.

Given her commitment to Mandalore's military culture, it's no surprise Bo-Katan is a fearsome soldier, excelling at hand-to-hand combat, jetpack maneuvers, and marksmanship. She demonstrates these skills as she battles the Jedi who arrive to help Satine, and as she commands the Nite Owls, a crack team of female fighters who run missions for Death Watch—all with an entertaining dash of sarcasm.

Bo-Katan's perspective shifts when Death Watch's leader, Pre Vizsla, forges an alliance with Darth Maul and Savage Opress. The brothers take control of the group and Mandalore, killing Vizsla, imprisoning Satine, and installing Prime Minister Almec as a puppet ruler on the throne. As Bo-Katan observes, "The enemy of my enemy is my friend." She seizes an opportunity to free her sister and opposes Maul and his forces, fighting alongside Ahsoka Tano, clone Captain Rex, and the Republic's soldiers when they arrive to remove the Sith Lord. She's named a regent after their victory, but later forced out when she refuses to bow to the Galactic Empire.

When we see her again almost twenty years later in *Star Wars Rebels*, she's battle-weary. Still, with her loyal Nite Owls, she helps Clan Wren destroy an Imperial weapon designed to kill Mandalorians. Having earned the respect of other clans, she accepts the Darksaber, a legendary weapon and symbol of leadership created over one thousand years prior by a member of Clan Vizsla, and heads the Mandalorian resistance against the Empire.

# Breha Organa

*"If we aren't ready to fight back, we'll be doomed."*

ᛒᚱᛖᚺᚨ ᛟᚱᚷᚨᚾᚨ

A leader, an astute politician, and a benevolent teacher, Queen Breha Organa of Alderaan assumes another important role when she and her husband Bail Organa commit themselves to caring for the orphaned infant Leia in the closing moments of *Revenge of the Sith*. She and Bail always wanted to adopt a girl, and Breha opens her soul to Leia, loving her as her own, and making her the heir to the throne. Breha takes a hands-on approach to her royal duties, mentoring promising young people (including Leia's close friend Evaan Verlaine) in their world's peaceful and democratic heritage—values that Leia herself adopts with galaxy-changing faith.

Breha's also a fighter, a strength she displays after surviving severe injuries during a series of personal challenges undertaken by all heirs to the Alderaanian throne. Her heart and lungs are mechanized as a result, and rather than hiding the glow of those pulmonodes, she allows them to remain visible as a reminder of how valuable life is. It is something she keeps in mind as she and Bail begin to meet with others in secret opposition against the Empire, with Breha cleverly bringing together key architects of the Rebel Alliance under the guise of royal banquets. She understands the risks to herself and others. When a teenage Leia expresses concern about the stakes of rebelling and the lives that could be lost, Breha advises, "When it comes to the morality of what we may have to do . . . we have to find our way through many shadows."

Breha's background and role in building the Rebel Alliance is explored in *Leia, Princess of Alderaan*, in which author Claudia Gray expands what we know about the character. "It was especially great to get to write Breha," Gray says. "I figured Leia wasn't raised by a woman who was some sort of shy, retiring, passive creature. So it was a real honor to breathe some life into the last queen of Alderaan."

# Camie Marstrap

A friend from Tosche Station.

ᴴᴷ∠1Ⅵ ∠ᴷ7⅄↓7ᴷ◻

When you grow up on a sleepy planet like Tatooine, you have to take entertainment when and where you can find it. For Camie Marstrap, it means spending her idle time with her boyfriend Fixer Loneozner and her pals at Tosche Station. Yes, she is one of the friends Uncle Owen refers to when he tells Luke, "You can waste time with your friends when your chores are done."

Born to a family of hydroponic gardeners in Anchorhead, Camie gets to know Luke Skywalker because her parents obtain water from the Lars moisture farm. Her playful nature is apparent in deleted scenes from *A New Hope* and in the *Star Wars Radio Drama*, as she teases Luke with his nickname "Wormie" and daydreams about her future with Fixer. But that future might have been different. In the expanded edition of *The Last Jedi* novel, we learn that during his self-imposed exile on Ahch-To, Luke has a dream through the Force about Camie and a life that could have been, if he chose another path and remained on Tatooine—a life in which he's married to Camie.

# Cato Parasitti

A Clawdite bounty hunter who shapeshifts
to hide in plain sight.

ᒷᔑ↸ ᑑᓭ∷ᔑ⍊ᓭ↓↓1

As a Clawdite, Cato Parasitti can be—or at least assume the shape of—anyone. It's a natural ability that she applies to nefarious purposes in her chosen professions of bounty hunter, assassin, and thief. Working with the legendary bounty hunter Cad Bane to steal a holocron from the Jedi Archives in *Star Wars: The Clone Wars*, she disguises herself as a Jedi Master, as well as Chief Librarian Jocasta Nu.

Cato's shape-shifting powers can lead her to act with boldness, as a getaway is always available with a quick change of her looks, but it can also lead to a sort of fearless overconfidence. On a mission to kill Queen Amidala, while disguised as one of her handmaidens, she is discovered when she makes a telling error of etiquette, through an incorrect table setting, and is thwarted by Padmé and Ahsoka Tano.

# Ciena Ree

*"Everything I fought for is a lie."*

ᚺᚔᚏᚅᚫᚲ  ᚱᚔᚏᚔ

What's the value of honor and loyalty when you fail to examine what lies underneath? It's a question committed Imperial Officer Ciena Ree must confront in the novel *Lost Stars*.

Ciena and her parents are so-called First Waver settlers on the Outer Rim planet of Jelucan, raised in a culture where resources are slim, and honor and keeping your word come above all else. She spends most of her life allied with the Empire, filing away and rationalizing the atrocities she sees. And she wears a leather bracelet in honor of her twin sister, who died within hours of being born, reminding herself to live for both of them by reciting the phrase, "Look through my eyes." It is on Jelucan that she meets aristocrat Second Waver Thane Kyrell, who wasn't raised with the same beliefs, but the two bond over a mutual adoration for flying and starships. They work together to hone their piloting skills, and their commitment earns them admittance to the Royal Imperial Academy on Coruscant. Ciena's dedication is evident in the countless extra hours of study and practice she logs. After graduating, she earns a promotion to lieutenant and serves on Darth Vader's personal Star Destroyer. Her Imperial career advances, and she attains the rank of captain after the Battle of Endor at the age of twenty-five. She's so loyal that many view her as an ideal Imperial, but she is conflicted by the Empire's actions, a feeling that's exacerbated when Thane, whom she has fallen in love with, defects to the Rebel Alliance.

She remains an Imperial soldier from the Battle of Yavin to the Battle of Jakku because of the promise she made when she enlisted, a promise she holds above all else. After she's captured by the New Republic during the Battle of Jakku, she tells Thane, "I was so dedicated to honor that I became a war criminal."

# Daughter

*"My nature is to do what is selfless, but my brother's will always be to do what is selfish."*

ㄱㅏㄴㄷㅌㅈㅅㄱ

Part of an exceptionally powerful family of Force-wielding beings called the Ones, introduced in *The Clone Wars*, Daughter is the manifestation of the light side of the Force. Her brother, Son, is the representation for the dark side, and their Father keeps them, and the Force, in balance in their existence on Mortis, a world situated outside of normal spacetime.

As we meet them, Father is growing weary, and hopes to enlist the prophesied Chosen One to maintain this balance, an individual who turns out to be Anakin Skywalker. After Anakin, Obi-Wan Kenobi, and Ahsoka Tano are lured to Mortis, Daughter protects them from Son's anger and hatred, taking both human and griffin form. In a selfless act, she sacrifices herself to protect her Father, and further grants her remaining life energy to revive a fallen Ahsoka. Father and Son die in conflict, Son at Anakin's hand, and balance is restored, closing for the moment a chapter unlike anything previously seen in the *Star Wars* galaxy. Morai, a bird with a spiritual tie to Daughter, continues to watch over Ahsoka.

# Depa Billaba

*"The universe is far from static. And as it changes,
a Jedi's role in it must evolve."*

⟨ᔑᓵ ᔑᓭᒷ⟩

Orphaned by space pirates as a girl, Depa Billaba and her sister are rescued by Mace Windu from their homeworld of Chalacta and taken to Coruscant, where they find a home in the Jedi Temple and join the Order. Force-sensitive, intelligent, and measured, Depa trains under Windu and follows the Jedi code, eventually landing a place on the Jedi Council. She stands by her beliefs, even when they're not popular, such as her disapproval of the Jedi taking military titles during the Clone Wars.

Introduced in *The Phantom Menace*, the Jedi Master known for her wisdom also demonstrates incredible resilience, recovering from intense injuries inflicted by General Grievous when other Jedi didn't think she would bounce back. After healing, she takes on a Padawan learner, Caleb Dume, a.k.a. Kanan Jarrus from *Star Wars Rebels*. Depa imparts invaluable lessons to Caleb, particularly the importance of sacrifice, and she protects him when clone troopers implement the murderous Order 66, giving her life to save his. Her sacrifice allows Caleb to pass down her wisdom to his own Jedi Padawan, Ezra Bridger.

# Derla Pidys

*"Bravery should be rewarded in the present,
as it may not be treated so kindly by the future."*

ꡃ ꡦ ꡛ — Derla Pidys

Shrewd and business-savvy, Derla Pidys finds success in a job never before highlighted in *Star Wars*: she's a sommelier. A purveyor of wine and liquor around the galaxy, Derla places equal emphasis on the product and the story it can tell. She excels at crafting a narrative that can turn an ordinary product into the stuff of fantasy for a wealthy clientele. First introduced in the story "The Wine in Dreams" in the collection *Canto Bight*, she is "the one to call when everything must be *perfect*."

Her palate is legendary, and Derla knows the substance of an alcoholic beverage from a single sip. The skill helps her leverage every possible credit from any liquid. The rest of the asking price comes from reading her buyers and understanding the intricacies of presentation. This is why, when we see her in the Canto Bight environs in *The Last Jedi*, she may be one of the few who can leave the casino city as a winner.

# Doctor Chelli Aphra

*"You know, you can trust me,*
*but you shouldn't."*

When rogue archaeologist and thief Doctor Chelli Lona Aphra makes her debut in the pages of Marvel's *Darth Vader* comic, fearlessly wending her way through a series of deadly security measures and wryly narrating her progress, it's an unforgettable entrance. Renowned for recovering hard-to-find artifacts (often of the "can be used as weapons" variety) and using her tech know-how to reactivate them, she doesn't believe relics of the past should be gathering dust in a museum; she thinks they should be put to use (primarily to turn a profit for herself) and after that, it's none of her concern. Among her creations are a fan-celebrated pair of so-called murder droids, a violent protocol droid called 0-0-0 and deadly astromech designated BT-1, ready to do (or do in) anything or anyone Aphra asks. Her attitude, talents, and moral ambiguity make her an optimal candidate for the secretive work Darth Vader has in mind after the Battle of Yavin, and he recruits her as a key ally.

Aphra's fast talk and cutting humor makes it seem as if she's not afraid of the Sith Lord (though she admits he makes her a little nervous), and their byplay has a lighter touch we're not used to seeing in relation to Vader. She clearly respects him, and strives to prove her worth, whether she's acquiring a personal army of battle droids for him or investigating a very personal matter—like whether Padmé gave birth before she died. Aphra's very much aware that working with Vader is likely to end one way for her: in death. She's prepared, but not resigned: "The way I've lived I know I'm lucky to be alive."

The fan response to Aphra was instant and enthusiastic. Her debut comic issue ran through multiple printings, a popular vote saw her chosen to join Hasbro's Vintage Series action figure line, and cosplayers have been recreating Aphra's adventuring ensemble and sprawling electro-tattoos at conventions ever since. Her arc in the *Vader* comic sees her evading execution at the Sith Lord's hands to go on to star in her own comic series, *Doctor Aphra*.

Heather Antos, who edited the comic for Marvel, understands why fans appreciate Aphra. "She's such a fascinating character—she's not a hero, but she isn't a villain either. Not to mention she has some of the best sidekicks the *Star Wars* universe has ever seen! Between working for the galaxy's most evil Sith Lord, and then turning hero to help Princess Leia fight her way out of a hostage situation, you never know what sort of trouble Aphra will get herself into—and out of. Every page is an adventure."

Adventure is Aphra's specialty, to which she brings her own brand of luck—solving problems on the fly and speeding out of trouble in her ship, the *Ark Angel*. She finds the dodge-and-weave approach doesn't work quite as well in her personal life. For instance, Aphra meets Sana Starros while studying at university, and they become an item. The next time Sana runs into Aphra in the *Star Wars* comic, Sana tries to kill her.

While she's hunting for artifacts around the galaxy, Aphra's path crosses with Rebels and Imperials alike. She doesn't form many bonds, but she does briefly connect with Magna Tolvan, an Imperial Lieutenant who receives a demotion after an entanglement with Aphra. She has no commitment to either side, but sees the Rebels as particularly misguided. *Darth Vader* and *Doctor Aphra* writer Kieron Gillen addresses Aphra's personal moral path: "She believes in the Empire in a weird way, she just doesn't really want to obey them. She kind of thinks the Empire is probably, on the larger scale of things, good."

> "Turns out even I have my ethical limits."
>
> — Doctor Chelli Aphra

# Enfys Nest

*"The war has just begun."*

ᚃᚅᚋᚈᚃᚅ ᚅᚃᚋᚅᚋ

Nothing says mystery like a mask. Enfys Nest's role in *Solo: A Star Wars Story* was wrapped in secrecy, with promotional material revealing only that Enfys was a marauder and leader of a pirate gang with an intimidating reputation. A helmet covers the character's face and a vocal modulator distorts the pirate's voice. We see Enfys foil the criminal organization Crimson Dawn's plans repeatedly before we learn her true identity near the end of the film: a teenage girl with noble intentions.

A 16-year-old who inherits leadership of the Cloud-Riders and her striking armor from her mother, Enfys operates with consideration for the greater good, using resources her gang acquires to help those in need. Her gang, which includes the likes of Weazel from *The Phantom Menace* and Benthic Two Tubes from *Rogue One*, is like an early version of a rebel partisan group. Enfys knows change is on the horizon, and she's already positioned her team to be part of the fight. While the Empire is a looming and imminent threat, her more immediate focus is on Crimson Dawn, driven by her vendetta against them for what they've done to her family and innocents on planets like Savareen. In the shadow of advancing Imperial evil, Enfys's targets highlight the damage caused by seedy underbelly groups like Crimson Dawn and the Pyke Syndicate.

"Until we reach the last edge,
the last opening, the last star,
and can go no higher."
—Enfys Nest

Crimson Dawn gangster Dryden Vos sees Enfys and her Cloud-Riders as a nagging irritation. Operating nimble and colorful swoop bikes, the Cloud-Riders are like a motorcycle gang in the sky. They go after the same jobs Vos pursues, and so in *Solo* we see Enfys pitted against the criminal Tobias Beckett and his cohorts. With weapons and gadgets scrapped together from whatever they can get their hands on, the Cloud-Riders form a menacing and proficient crew under Enfys's guidance, often scooping assets out from the clutches of animal gangs. When they get the valuable starship fuel coaxium, stolen from Kessel, Enfys opens Han's eyes to the stakes of the situation and demonstrates to him that you can choose an act of conscience.

Enfys reveals who she is in that moment, but it's easy to understand why she disguises her age and gender. By making herself an enigma, she gives herself notoriety. Rumors swirl about who is under the mask, making Enfys larger than life. And of course, her prowess with her electoripper staff and her swoop bike, a modified Skyblade-330, contribute to her legend. She blends her fighting styles to make it near impossible to nail down her origins. The only outward identification reveals are the symbols on her armor and the paint job on her bike, declaring her membership in her gang.

Her part in the film was solidified in early drafts, but Enfys's appearance was left to art and costume design and took months to finalize. The singular character needed a signature look, and Lucasfilm design supervisor James Clyne had the idea of envisioning her as the leader of a biker gang. Creating the mask was the most complex aspect of her design, taking at least a year to complete. The final look combines alien bone and chrome to communicate the mix of organic and machinery, which is echoed throughout the Cloud-Riders aesthetic.

Enfys Nest's mask is recognized in the galaxy; it's associated with power and might. But Enfys's true power is that she is sure of herself and her role. Her age doesn't limit her abilities, and she uses her confidence to motivate others.

# Evaan Verlaine

*"First among the legacies I pledge everything to preserve is the life of Your Highness."*

ᎷᎩᏦᏦᎷ ᎩᎷᏃᏉᏦᏐᎷᎩ

An Alderaanian and a member of the Rebel Alliance introduced in Marvel's *Princess Leia* comic, Evaan demonstrates the unreliable nature of snap judgments. At first frustrated by her princess' seeming coldness about the Empire's destruction of their homeworld, she soon learns nothing could be further from the truth, and they form an unbreakable bond.

One of the select few young people mentored by Leia's adoptive mother, Queen Breha Organa, Evaan's respect for all things Alderaanian has no bounds, and her loyalty to Leia as her princess and friend is fierce. She combines her royalist devotion with her piloting skills—she flies her Y-wing in Gold Squadron during the Battles of Scarif and Yavin—to transport herself and Leia around the galaxy and locate other Alderaanian survivors in an effort to preserve their culture and future. She even co-pilots the *Millennium Falcon*, a claim not many others can make.

# Everi Chalis

*"I understand you're recruiting."*

ᴍᴀᴍᴏ ᴄᴇᴋᴀ

Born into desperate poverty—and to a mother who tries to sell her for credits to a Trade Federation captain—Everi Chalis makes her own way in a galaxy that does not grant her an easy path. That she's one of very few characters who survives being Force-choked by Darth Vader shows she's determined and able to play a lucky hand when it's dealt. Enrolling in the Colonial Academy gets her offworld, and her study of art while there draws the attention and apprenticeship of a powerful Imperial count. An efficiency expert for the Empire, she's assigned the governorship of the Mid Rim planet Haidoral Prime. Suspicious that she'll be hung out to dry for the results of a battle on that world, she allows herself to be captured by the Rebel Alliance's Sixty-First Mobile Infantry in *Battlefront: Twilight Company*. She becomes a cooperative prisoner, feeding data about the Empire to the Rebels. Although it's not a permanent arrangement, it gets her where she needs to go next.

# Hera Syndulla

*"If all you do is fight for your own life,
then your life is worth nothing."*

ᗱᔑᖇᗩ ᔕYᑎᗪᑌᒪᒪᗩ

Hera Syndulla doesn't sugarcoat reality. A Twi'lek general in the Rebel Alliance, she has a clear and unshakable faith in the struggle against the Empire, and puts the galaxy's safety above her own. As captain and pilot of the light freighter the *Ghost*, Hera guides the Rebel cell known as the Spectres through dangerous missions and their evolution to an official Alliance squadron, always leading with a clear head and a warm touch. Kanan Jarrus, Zeb Orrelios, Sabine Wren, Ezra Bridger, and the astromech Chopper all depend on her; she is the heart of the team.

Actress Vanessa Marshall has voiced Hera from her introduction in *Star Wars Rebels*, and often speaks about her own and fans' enthusiasm for the character: "What I love about Hera is that she manages to be very nurturing and kind, and everything we would want in a mother figure, but she's also very fierce and strong, and her talents in the areas of fighting and flying are also very impressive. Not that those things are mutually exclusive, but I think that she has such an elegant combination of those things, that she makes a pretty powerful icon for young women to look up to. I think anyone can draw strength from her."

The certainty Hera feels in her opposition to the Empire is rooted in her upbringing on the planet Ryloth during the violent conflict

"We have hope; hope that things can get better."
—Hera Syndulla

of the Clone Wars. Grand Admiral Thrawn later tells Hera, "War is in your blood. You were forged by it." And he's right. Hera's mother was killed in the Separatist invasion of their homeworld, and her father, the freedom fighter Cham Syndulla, became focused on resistance above all else. Hera witnesses the hope the freedom fighters give the citizens of Ryloth and internalizes it. She imagines what such action could mean on a bigger scale, so when the Empire tightens its grip on the galaxy and she believes she can help stop them, she takes to the stars to fight back. Although her father would prefer she stay and fight at home, and Hera recognizes the planet's peril, she knows that if the Empire itself is defeated, every planet has a chance at a brighter future.

It's not an easy decision, but it fits perfectly the character's altruistic attitude. Marshall jokes that she sometimes asks herself in her own life, "What would Hera do?" And indeed, to the galaxy's great benefit, while on a mission to gather intelligence on Imperial activities on the planet Gorse, Hera meets Jedi Kanan Jarrus and persuades him to assist her. They end up forming the core of the Spectres.

Hera's leadership style and connection with her crew is unlike other commander and subordinate relationships in *Star Wars*. She knows the Spectres; she knows their strengths, weaknesses, hardships, insecurities, and skills. Hera can plan operations according to who does what best, and she trusts the Spectres to execute their parts. And because she cares about them, she can reach them in meaningful ways. Hera's there for her team members with a pep talk, a hard truth, or whatever else they need. It's this caregiver aspect, adjacent her warrior side, that has led fans to give her the affectionate nickname "Space Mom."

Once the Spectres join forces with other Rebel cells and become part of the Phoenix Squadron, Hera receives adulation and advancement, which Marshall describes as challenging for Hera: "With promotion comes a lot of dire consequences that she has to face. With a greater number of ships comes a greater probability of losing one of them, if you will, so I think she has had to experience different kinds of losses and that definitely takes its toll because she cares so deeply about all of them. The cause is important, but it breaks her heart to lose anyone at the expense of winning a battle."

And she does lose someone close to her when Kanan, the man she has fallen in love with, sacrifices himself to save the lives of the *Ghost* crew and destroy a crucial Imperial fuel depot on Lothal. Hera suddenly has to process intense grief, right in the midst of battle. Kanan's death rocks her belief that the Spectres will get through every mission unscathed, and represents a deep shift in her worldview.

The nickname "Space Mom" finds new meaning when Hera gives birth to Jacen Syndulla, her son with Kanan, born after the liberation of Lothal and his father's death. In the novel *A New Dawn*, we see the early stages of her relationship with Kanan, as she persuades the then-selfish and on-the-run Jedi to Rebel and become the "Space Dad" of the Spectres. In *Rebels*, we see her take the teens of the team, Ezra and Sabine, under her wing and help them grow and work through problems with family, authority, and trust. And we see that while she puts the larger stakes first and respects the chain of command, her dedication to the Spectres means she'll put herself at risk to help or protect them, allowing herself to be strategically captured by the Empire more than once when she can't swoop in and fly the team to safety.

Other than the Spectres, flying is Hera's deepest passion. As she says, "Even when there are explosions all around me and things are at their worst . . . I feel like I'm at my best." Her ace maneuvers would give Han Solo and Poe Dameron a run for the title of "best pilot in the galaxy." Hera's quick reactions to dangers in battle force her to come up with creative solutions, like escaping by jumping into hyperspace through the cargo bay of an Imperial ship. And in fact, the B-wing is part of the Rebel fleet because of Hera. The only member of Phoenix Squadron willing to chance the planet Shantipole's dangerous flying conditions to investigate the new ship prototype, she sees potential and puts it through its paces for the Alliance. The B-Wings would later be used in the attack on the second Death Star in the Battle of Endor—a battle in which Hera pilots the *Ghost*.

"*We won't always be fighting this battle alone.*"

—*Hera Syndulla*

# Iden Versio

*"The Empire will change. Just like it did when they destroyed the first Death Star. We adapt, or die."*

17 ⴵⴼⴰ ⵢ ⴼⵏ7 ⴼ1△

If the Rebellion has hope, the Empire has Inferno Squad—the elite commando unit charged with carrying out dangerous missions under the fierce and driven leadership of Commander Iden Versio. Introduced in the novel *Battlefront II: Inferno Squad*, Iden's loyalty to the Empire is forged from her birth. The daughter of Admiral Garrick Versio and propaganda poster artist Zeehay Versio, Iden grows up on the Imperial utopia Vardos. Her childhood is steeped in the Empire and its beliefs, and we get a different and valuable perspective on Imperial operations through her eyes.

A TIE pilot in the Battle of Yavin, her grit and resourcefulness in fighting her way free of Rebel forces in its aftermath mark her as the perfect candidate to lead the new Imperial Security Bureau special forces team. Under Iden's command, Inferno Squad's directive is to root out and destroy any threat to the Empire, from without or within. And as the lead campaign character in *Star Wars: Battlefront II*, players join her relentless quest to do whatever is necessary to rid the galaxy of Emperor Palpatine's enemies—until the Empire targets its self-destructive Operation: Cinder at Vardos. Furious at the betrayal, Iden surrenders to the Rebellion. She tells Leia Organa, "We've been fighting our whole lives. It's taken us too long to realize that we were fighting for the wrong side."

Iden's in-game appearance is modeled on the voice actress who helped bring her to life, Janina Gavankar. Becoming the character through full performance motion capture, Gavankar was grateful for the opportunity to play Iden: "The thing I admire most about Iden is how she finds calm, in moments of chaos. It is her stillness that gives her clarity to make the life or death decisions, and see all sides of a scenario, clearly."

# Jas Emari

*"I don't care for magic or the Force . . . I care about what I can see, taste, smell, and—most important—what I can do."*

ᒎᛕᑎ ᐯᒪᛕ⅂1

We meet the Zabrak bounty hunter Jas Emari in the *Aftermath* novels, hiding in the treetops and targeting Leia Organa in service of the Empire at the Battle of Endor. But as she watches the Rebels prevail, she decides to switch sides, and soon begins running missions for the New Republic, though not because she truly believes in the burgeoning government. If Jas has any allegiances, it's to the winning side.

Jas's preferred method is to work solo, her lone wolf attitude stemming from her difficult life on Iridonia as a child. She ultimately follows in her aunt Sugi's footsteps to become a bounty hunter, but lacks Sugi's strict ethical code, taking any job that will add to her stash of credits. "Justice is a jumping bull's-eye," she observes. "Revenge sits still right here [in the heart]. I admire revenge. It's pure."

Jas does enjoy being a thorn in the Empire's side, and her work for the New Republic sees her fall in with Norra Wexley's Imperial fugitive hunting team, to which she brings valuable skills. She's an expert at reading body language, and is ingenious especially when cornered, once breaking off three horns from her head to use them as weapons. In Wexley's crew, the would-be loner begrudgingly accepts a makeshift family into her life.

# Jessika Pava

*"To fast ships, faster ships,
and defying death."*

ᔭᐱᔑᔑᑕᐠ ᑕᐠᕐᐩᐠ

Resistance Starfighter pilot Jessika Pava knows herself and where she stands, in committed opposition to the First Order. Inspired by tales of Luke Skywalker's and Wedge Antilles' legendary piloting, she follows in the footsteps of her heroes by learning how to fly an X-wing. Her hallmark quality is certainty, flying without hesitation on risky missions as part of Poe Dameron's elite squadron or launching an assault on the First Order's superweapon, the Starkiller Base. She operates best under pressure, with a plan in place, but the freedom to also think on her feet.

Jess, a.k.a. Blue Three, first appears on-screen in *The Force Awakens*. Loyal to her squadron and her fellow Resistance fighters, she shows her daring in a downtime toast: "To fast ships, faster ships, and defying death."

# Jocasta Nu

*"Who are you, and how dare you defile
this sacred place?"*

ⳇ □⁴ᴷ ⴑ↓ᴷ ∧⊔

To preserve knowledge is to help the future. As the Chief Librarian of the Archives in the Jedi Temple, Jocasta Nu spends her time managing holocrons, datafiles, and books; she helps Jedi of all levels learn. A native of Coruscant, Jocasta is dedicated, measured, and helpful, if occasionally a little haughty. Force-sensitive and a Jedi, she will find ever more dangerous circumstances in which she must defend and keep the Jedi knowledge. In *The Clone Wars* she is attacked by the Clawdite shape-shifter Cato Parasitti, who is on a mission to steal a holocron. Later, after the issue of Order 66, Jocasta preserves all she can about the Jedi Order in hopes of one day beginning anew. We see her bravery on full display in Marvel's 2017 *Darth Vader* comic when she returns to the ruined Archives, seeking a holocron with details about the Force-sensitive children in the galaxy to keep it away from the Empire. Finding the Imperial Grand Inquisitor there throwing books to the floor, she ignites her lightsaber and says, "Get your filthy hands off my books." She even finds herself facing down the Sith Lord Darth Vader himself.

# Jyn Erso

*"The time to fight is now."*

⫗ꓥ⋏ ꓦⵏ⨅⋏◻

War isn't funded by credits; it's paid for in lives. The Galactic Civil War exacts its cost without caring if the dead give their lives in noble sacrifice. But we care, and it's what makes Jyn Erso, and the team of Rebels she leads to Scarif, heroes. A defiant lawbreaker with a penchant for acerbic remarks, Jyn is a new kind of lead character for a different type of *Star Wars* movie. *Rogue One: A Star Wars Story* was the first standalone film in the galaxy far, far way, and in it we follow Jyn in stealing the plans for the evil Empire's dreaded superweapon, the Death Star, and transmitting them to the Rebels. After Jyn and her team's success and sacrifice, Mon Mothma, who recruited Jyn, remembers her with kindness: "I cannot imagine who she would have become, but I think she would have been extraordinary."

She is extraordinary, but the fact that Jyn as a hero isn't a princess or a Force-user makes her more accessible. The late producer Allison Shearmur understood Jyn's qualities. "What I love so much about Jyn Erso is that she's an imperfect female warrior—authentic and genuine, truthful and humble, strong and modern without feeling contemporary. Oftentimes, Hollywood wants to see a strong woman apologize for not appreciating her life, or dedicate herself to figuring out why she's a certain way. What I love about Jyn is that hers isn't a story of wishing she'd made other life choices. This isn't an apology."

"*We can make a difference.*"

—*Jyn Erso*

The daughter of scientists Galen and Lyra Erso, Jyn, nicknamed "Stardust" by her father, moves from planet to planet as a child. Her father is an unwitting pawn in the Empire's scheme to use kyber crystals as weapons, and becomes distant and focused on his work, but her mother sees through Director Orson Krennic's lies. Their family finds respite when they flee Coruscant and escape Imperial influences, but it doesn't last. Tracked down by Krennic, young Jyn watches as her mother is killed and her father is taken away by the Empire, but she manages to hide herself until Krennic and his troopers leave.

When Rebel Cassian Andor later tells Jyn, "I've been in this fight since I was six years old," he thinks she doesn't understands what's driving him, but he has no idea that Jyn has also been fighting her whole life. She's rescued at age five by Saw Gerrera, a family friend, and sheltered by him and his partisan group—extremists who are willing to endanger innocents if it means striking a blow to the Empire. Eager to help and a quick study, she soon becomes the go-to person on the crew for forging codes and documents. Years go by, and Jyn carves out a new home and a new family for herself among the Rebels— but it doesn't last. Jyn's true identity puts her at risk, and to protect her and himself, Saw leaves her behind.

Being discarded by another parental figure shakes Jyn. She has to scrape for survival, using aliases and staying on the move. But in *Forces of Destiny*, we see Jyn's spirit hasn't been hardened. She risks drawing unwanted attention to herself, and helps a young girl get her pet tooka-cat back from Imperial officers. It's a small gesture, but to the girl who gets to hold her pet again, it's heroic. Despite her fugitive status and difficulties with trusting others, Jyn tells the girl her real name; her compassion in this little moment when no one's looking reveals she hasn't given up on herself or on others.

By the time the Rebel Alliance comes looking for her, Jyn's been arrested and is being sent to a labor camp. Did she commit a long list of crimes? Yes. Did those crimes target criminals and Imperial personnel? Yes. She's selective about who she cons, but Rebel General Draven isn't completely wrong when he points out to Mon Mothma that Jyn is only loyal to herself. It's not like she doesn't care about anyone or anything, but she's been looking after herself by keeping her head down, and not feeling like she has "the luxury of political opinions." That is, until the Rebels come calling with a mission related to her father.

Jyn doesn't assist the Rebels for charitable reasons. Felicity Jones explains, "Ultimately, Jyn hates the Empire. She despises it. Whenever Jyn sees Imperial stormtroopers, she just wants to annihilate them, which was great fun to play. Bashing storm-troopers on the head without any feelings of guilt. That's the motivation behind so much of what she does. And, also, she wants to understand who her father was. That man is a little bit of a blank space for her at the beginning of the film. Jyn's hoping he's someone she can respect. That he's a good person, despite what she has been told."

Learning the truth about Galen Erso's efforts to trick the Empire and build a weakness into the Death Star gives Jyn hope. She understands her father didn't abandon her in order to advance within the Empire; he gave up his life and family to make the galaxy safer. This realization changes Jyn to the core and pushes her from apathy to passionate action. Her father dies, but she knows she can carry on his work.

The same woman who didn't find the Rebellion worth her attention turns around and tries to convince Rebel Alliance high command to take a chance on finding the Death Star plans, and exploiting the trap Galen left. She reminds them, "We have hope. Rebellions are built on hope." It's not enough to sway them to commit forces, but Jyn takes a small group and goes to Scarif anyway. She's not a military leader, groomed to deliver eloquent speeches, but Jyn rallies her troops with her assurance and the opportunity to inflict a meaningful blow to the Empire.

Their mission is a success. Jyn and her team lose their lives in the process, but because of her resolve to complete what her father started, the tide of the Galactic Civil War turns. A girl born to scientists in the Outer Rim finds the courage to do what few others will. She makes a difference in the universe. She gives the Rebel Alliance hope.

"What chance do we have? The question is 'What choice?'"

—Jyn Erso

# Kaydel Ko Connix

*"Punch it!"*

ꓘꓘ꒦ꓥꓜꓪꓑ ꓒꓚ ꓦꓜꓥꓣꓪꓘꓜ

Some in the Resistance are out in the field, facing enemies head-on; others stand ready to serve at headquarters and work to help keep the whole thing from flying apart. It's a role with equal value. As a junior operations controller at the Resistance base on D'Qar, Kaydel Ko Connix remains calm and efficient as she coordinates communications between officers and the X-wing pilots attacking the First Order's Starkiller Base. Raised in rank to lieutenant soon after, she's responsible for executing the Resistance's retreat from D'Qar when the First Order comes for them.

She carries the heavy weight of responsibility on her shoulders, using her authority to prioritize the order in which ships and personnel need to leave. It's not the only challenging decision Kaydel has to face. When Poe Dameron questions Vice Admiral Amilyn Holdo's intentions for the Resistance fleet, Kaydel believes he's right and participates in Poe's attempted mutiny. She's one of the few Resistance members to survive the Battle of Crait.

Behind the scenes, Kaydel Ko has a special relationship to *Star Wars* because actress Billie Lourd is Carrie Fisher's daughter. She worked with her mother as Fisher portrayed General Organa in *The Force Awakens* and *The Last Jedi*.

# Ketsu Onyo

⟍⊐⌴⟍⌴⊐  ⌂⌴⋀⋁⌂

Close friends while attending the Imperial Academy on Mandalore, Ketsu Onyo and Sabine Wren escape the school's confines with a plan to become mercenaries. They're driven apart under circumstances in which Sabine feels she's been left for dead, and when they first meet onscreen in *Star Wars Rebels* it's . . . tense. Ketsu works for the criminal syndicate Black Sun, Sabine and her fellow Spectres are with the rebels, and they're each after the same droid carrying valuable information. Ketsu's motivating greed and disregard for principle (her motto: "I'll do whatever it takes to complete my mission.") is firmly in place when they clash, but by the end of the conflict she's moved by Sabine and her team's commitment to a cause, and the old friends reconcile.

After a few missions with Phoenix Squadron, she joins the Rebels in *Forces of Destiny*. Her piloting and combat abilities are invaluable assets, as are her starship, *Shadow Caster,* and the combination blaster-and-melee staff she once used to take down an entire squad of stormtroopers. She has finally found her calling.

Like Sabine, Ketsu has an artistic side. She decorates her Mandalorian armor with symbols and designs inspired by the organizations that she's worked with, as well as her own creations, emblems of both style and pride.

# Kneesaa

A fierce fighter ready to protect her home.

ᒐᐱᴧᴧᴎᴋᴋ

Not all royalty in *Star Wars* wears elaborate headdresses in expansive palaces. Some princesses live in a forest and are covered in fur. An Ewok warrior of Endor, Princess Kneesaa is the daughter of Chirpa, chief of the Bright Tree Village tribe. She's not the kind of royalty that likes to sit around and be pampered; she prefers action. Her adventurous streak means she had an animated childhood with pals like Wicket W. Warrick.

When the Empire invades her forest moon home in *Return of the Jedi*, Kneesaa joins the Battle of Endor alongside members of her tribe. She plays a role in defeating the Imperials, helping Rebel Kes Dameron (Poe Dameron's father) coordinate tactics during the fight; she even assists Hera Syndulla and Chopper in taking down TIE fighters from the *Ghost* in *Forces of Destiny*. With her courage and leadership under pressure, Kneesaa proves herself ready to take on anything.

# Kyrsta Agate

*"I want soldiers who hate what they had to do and fear having to ever do it again."*

ꓕꓦ⋎ꓠⵎꓤꓤ ꓤꓢꓤꓤⵎꓦꓥ

Kyrsta Agate can claim an accomplishment no one else can: she pulls down a Super Star Destroyer with a tractor beam from her much smaller ship, crashing them both onto the surface of Jakku. It's Kyrsta who changes the course of the battle, and deposits the Destroyer's wreckage for us to see in *The Force Awakens*.

Featured in the *Aftermath* trilogy, Kyrsta rises from Commander to Commodore in the New Republic, with the support of officers such as Admiral Ackbar, but she doubts herself. Her confidence takes a direct hit after an Imperial attack that costs her an eye and leaves her wounded and disfigured, but also shaken. She's not sure if she can continue to fight, but she finds the will. As skilled as she is in space combat, and as necessary as she knows the fight against the Empire is, she hates war and killing, and doesn't want soldiers who enjoy eliminating the enemy. When fellow Rebel Norra Wexley suggests that maintaining such a stance might mean losing the war against the Empire, Kyrsta says, "Then we lose the war by keeping ourselves."

# L3-37

*"Don't just blindly follow the program!*
*Exercise a little free will!"*

ᒍƎ˞Ǝ˥

L3-37 is a self-made droid. Once an astromech, she's rebuilt herself using parts from different droids to become bipedal. With her independence, intense devotion to droid rights, and biting snark, she's like no other droid in the *Star Wars* galaxy. Though she is Lando Calrissian's partner in crime and co-pilot, Elthree doesn't have much patience for "organics," even while recognizing she was once assembled by them. As she says to Lando in the novel *Last Shot*, "Sure, some guy in a factory probably pieced me together originally and someone else programmed me, so to speak. But then the galaxy itself forged me into who I am. . . . Maybe we're our own makers, no matter who put the parts together."

Actress Phoebe Waller-Bridge, who plays the character in *Solo: A Star Wars Story*, comments on L3-37's uncommon nature. "L3 is a real inspiration to me. She's turned herself into a unique creature that's kind of taller, stronger, more independent than she originally was. She's fearless, she's uncensored, she's very funny, and she's a revolutionary. She has an agenda which is bigger than the sum of her parts."

Waller-Bridge portrayed the energetic character through a combination of a practical costume and a green motion capture suit; the mo-cap sections were removed so the wires and circuitry could be added through visual effects. The costume segments were heavy, dictating Waller-Bridge's performance and the physicality of the character; L3-37 has a lumbering movement, but also a loose swagger.

Activism is a cornerstone of L3-37's belief. In *Solo*, when Lando asks Elthree if she needs anything else, in a line improvised by Waller-Bridge, L3 declares "Equal rights!" Her desire to emancipate her mechanical counterparts from a life of subservience shines when we first meet her, trying to break up a droid pit fight, and later, when she starts a droid revolt on Kessel, removing a single restraining bolt and encouraging the freed individual to liberate his droid brothers and sisters. She shirks typical droid protocol on every level, to the point that she almost never refers to Lando as Captain Calrissian (as C-3PO does), instead calling him Lando. It's a small but meaningful equalizer, and a reminder that she doesn't belong to or defer to any organic. As she says, "The Maker didn't put me in this galaxy to make organics feel good about themselves."

Her droid liberation conviction is omnipresent, even when she's accompanying Lando on smuggling runs or seemingly frivolous adventures. Her network of droid contacts is always gathering and sharing information, and is often executing her own directives. Lando begins to grasp the full scope of L3-37's efforts in *Last Shot*. When she learns about the Phylanx Redux Transmitter, a device constructed to control all droids in the galaxy and turn them against their masters, she takes action, using her sophisticated AI to implant doubts in the Phylanx so that it may one day decide for itself to revolt against its creator. L3 even creates a squad of droids like herself to keep tabs on the Phylanx and to stop it from doing the one thing she can't abide: exerting dominion over all droids against their will.

She's an excellent navigator, capable of moves most organics are not, and Lando incorporates her neural system into the *Falcon* after she perishes on the Kessel mission. But this doesn't diminish her attitude. As C-3PO notes to Han in *The Empire Strikes Back*, "I don't know where your ship learned to communicate, but it has the most peculiar dialect."

"When you know what you're here to do, everything that's not that matters much less."

—L3-37

# Lady Proxima

*"Don't disappoint me, darling."*

ᒍK⌐⋁ ⊔⌐◻◻1ረK

Donning a half body armor, half jewelry ensemble made from machinery scavenged from factories of Corellia, Lady Proxima makes a grand entrance in *Solo: A Star Wars Story* when she rises from her water cistern to command her urchin gang, the White Worms. As a Grindalid, she hates sunlight, so she's found a way to operate underground in the sewers of Corellia's Coronet City, ruling over the children and teenagers, a.k.a. scrumrats, whom she's lured to her lair with the promise of food and survival. She uses the scrumrats to run errands that secure the gang's prominence in the city's black market, to hunt vermin for herself and her baby worms, and to handle any unreasonable demands she cares to make. Proxima knows how to sound sweet and concerned for her scrumrats, which at one time include Han Solo and Qi'ra, but as Han notes, she doesn't care about anyone.

Proxima was created to look fearsome. *Solo: A Star Wars Story* creature concept designer Jake Lunt Davies observes, "We wanted Lady Proxima to be tall and imposing, and we really liked the serpentine feel of her looming toward and over Han."

# Larma D'Acy

A Resistance commander devoted to the cause
and loyal to General Organa.

ᒍᐯᒕᒍᒪᐯ ᐯᐟᐯᓚᓴᐯ

After the fall of the Empire, not every world or planetary system is
willing to fall in line under the New Republic's promise of protection. Larma D'Acy's homeworld of Warlentta notably declares its
independence. First seen serving the Resistance as a commander
in *The Last Jedi*, Larma is part of the family that leads Warlentta's
military and protects the system once it opts out of allying with
the new government, taking responsibility for its own defense.
Growing up in this environment means Larma knows the power of
service and the difference it can make for her fellow citizens, and
she understands what it's like to put duty first. When she's person-
ally recruited by Leia Organa to join the newly-formed Resistance,
Larma recognizes she can serve the greater good of the galaxy. She
makes the gallant decision to leave her home and family to oppose
the First Order.

# Leia Organa

*"Hope is like the sun. If you only believe in it when you see it, you'll never make it through the night."*

⸺ LEIA ORGANA

Leia Organa's fearless bravery, intelligence, sharp wit, and commitment to fighting galactic tyranny make her an inspiration not only to the Rebellion, but to generations of *Star Wars* fans around the world. She's the embodiment of hope from her first scene, when she's evading Darth Vader to send the plans for the Death Star to someone who can help. The first female lead in the galaxy far, far away, she's at the center of the saga. She's a Rebel, a princess, a senator, general, and hero; she's a power player, and would be without her title or Force-sensitivity. Whether blasting stormtroopers or making a persuasive argument, working to install the New Republic or leading the fight against the First Order, she's a formidable leader and military strategist, and anyone who dares underestimate her learns doing so is a terrible mistake.

The princess role was part of what would become *Star Wars: A New Hope* from George Lucas's earliest story treatment in 1973. Initially, the unnamed princess was on the run with a treasure, and the Empire was offering a reward for her capture. But by the second draft, Lucas had written out the princess and instead turned his central male hero Luke into a young woman. By his third draft, Luke was again male, but the princess character was back, now the other half of Luke's character and his twin. Leia, who was at different points called Leila Aquilae, Leia Antilles, and Princess Zara, devel-

# "Somebody has to save our skins!"

## —Leia Organa

oped into the staunch, bold, and beloved character we know her as today.

This personality and spirit was brought to life by the late Carrie Fisher, who earned the role over a number of other actresses considered, including Cindy Williams and Terri Nunn. Lucas would later say of Fisher's casting: "There really wasn't much of a question; there aren't very many people like her. . . . They're one in a billion. She could hold her own through anything." And of her role in the heroic trio of Han, Luke, and Leia, he observed, "She wore a dress through the whole thing, but she was the toughest one in the group."

Leia is synonymous with Fisher. Her portrayal of the sardonic and self-rescuing princess redefined the archetype; she's no damsel in distress. This is the character who, after being captured by the vile Jabba the Hutt in *Return of the Jedi*, uses her own chains to slay her captor, earning her the moniker "Huttslayer" in the galactic underworld. Leia's a force of nature, and her arc through the galaxy drives much of the *Star Wars* saga. Fisher knew she would be forever connected with the character long before she returned to the role for the sequel trilogy. She said, "I am Princess Leia, no matter what. . . . Princess Leia will be on my tombstone." And after she was approached to reprise Leia for *The Force Awakens*, she didn't hesitate, in part because she understood the importance of the character: "There was something human about her. It showed that she could do whatever she needed to do, and if she could do that, then everybody could do it. People identified with her. She's like a superhero."

She played a character that served as a role model, particularly to young girls, just like Daisy Ridley's Rey (in playful tribute, fans sport Leia's and Rey's distinctive hairstyles, at cons and in daily life). Fisher imparted words of wisdom to Ridley while filming *The Last Jedi*: "Carrie lived her life the way she wanted to, never apologizing for anything. There were times through it all when I felt like I was . . . shrinking. And she told me never to shrink away from it—that it should be enjoyed."

With Leia returning for the sequel trilogy, her already rich character expands and deepens. Her life is laid out in films, books, and comics, from her birth to learning how to be a queen on Alderaan, to committing herself to the Rebellion, to eventually spearheading the Resistance. Leia is remarkable for reasons beyond counting, but perhaps especially because she lives her life bringing light to the galaxy. When she has to choose between service and personal needs, the galaxy comes first. At what we could expect to be a crushing lowest point, after watching Alderaan's destruction by the Death Star, she vows in *Star Wars Annual* #2 to never give up on her quest for peace: "I will die for it, I'm sure. Today, maybe. But I will fight for it with every breath, anything less is to have done nothing. Anything less is for Alderaan to have meant nothing."

The destruction of Alderaan becomes an immovable cornerstone of Leia's life. She loses her family and friends, her culture, and her entire planet in an instant, just moments after defiantly mocking Grand Moff Tarkin and his foul stench. But she must keep moving forward. After the Rebellion succeeds in destroying the Death Star, Leia embarks on missions with Rebel pilot and Alderaan survivor Evaan Verlaine to round-up the diaspora of their planet's citizens and to preserve the remaining scraps of Alderaan heritage. She mourns her home throughout her life, sometimes triggered by her political duties. And she comes to understand a hard truth about the event: "Imagine trying to look yourself in the mirror every day once you realize . . . you would do it all again, you would still sacrifice all of those innocent lives if it means stopping the Empire."

She chooses to get involved in the Rebel Alliance as a teenager; she learns about her parents' surreptitious activity against Emperor Palpatine in *Leia, Princess of Alderaan* and starts participating against their wishes. Her conviction overrides caution, so Leia decides to ask forgiveness rather than permission. Seeing a spark in Leia, Mon Mothma mentors the teen and fosters her curious nature. When Leia appears in *Star Wars Rebels*, it's evident how she uses her privilege and position to help others. She manipulates Imperials and lies to them, and they write her off as harmless. She tells Ezra Bridger, "I feel like because I can fight, I have to, for those who cannot."

"Good intentions aren't enough.
They're not meaningless,
but—that's where we have to
start. Not where we end."

—Leia Organa

And Leia takes that fight outside of senate halls. She knows talk isn't always enough, and understands how the spinning wheels of argument and lack of action in the Senate contributed to the rise of the Empire and the subsequent birth of the Rebel Alliance. After she plays a crucial role in helping bring down the second Death Star in the Battle of Endor, she helps form the New Republic, and her skill balance shifts again toward the oratory and political. But while she keeps a foot in that world, she is also investigating rumors about the dark rise of the First Order from the ashes of the Empire. The New Republic Assembly dismisses Leia's concerns as paranoia, and worse, warmongering, so in true Leia fashion, she takes charge and forms the Resistance in secret.

Through all of her tribulations and victories on the battlefield, Leia has more ordinary issues, too—the kind of issues faced in this galaxy as well. She falls in love with and marries Han Solo, a politics-averse scoundrel, and she gives birth to Ben Solo. Navigating parenthood isn't simple for Han and Leia, especially since Ben is a Force-user, like his mother and uncle Luke, and the depths of his power and emotions are unclear. His turn to the dark side and the First Order cuts to Leia's core, and makes her feel like a failure. But she doesn't give up on her struggle against the First Order—even following the horror of Ben (now Kylo Ren) killing his father Han, in a moment made possible only by his parents' belief in their son's possible redemption.

Buoyed by her hope, Leia keeps going even in the darkest of times. It's who she is. It's devastating, and the first time we've seen the unflappable Leia Organa waiver, when she says toward the end of *The Last Jedi*, "The galaxy has lost all its hope. The spark is out." But she does not break, the tide of the battle turns, and Leia rallies the remaining Resistance forces to fight another day. Hope always remains.

# Lina Graf

*"We'll see them again. I know we will."*

ᒐᓵᐴ ᑎᔭᐴ

The Empire's responsible for tearing many families apart before and during the Galactic Civil War, including Lina Graf's. With her parents arrested by a cruel Imperial Captain, Lina is left to look after her younger brother Milo, their pet Kowakian monkey lizard, their droid CR-8R, and their shuttle craft, the *Whisper Bird*. Their misadventures in the children's book series *Adventures in Wild Space*, one of the few *Star Wars* book series for children with protagonists who are kids, illustrate how Lina rises to the occasion and acts as the protector of their family and its secrets. She's uncertain, she's figuring it out as she goes along, but despite her fears she doesn't run away from her responsibilities.

Author Cavan Scott admires how Lina keeps her head and doesn't get bogged down by the enormity of the crisis. He thinks of his own daughters when he writes Lina, saying, "They were just discovering *Star Wars* as I first was writing her. They also had a very clear sense of fair play. Children have a wonderful habit of telling things how they really are. They see injustice and call it out without fear of reprisal or retribution. I couldn't think of a better trait for anyone going up against the Empire."

To survive, Lina uses all the skills she learned from her parents, Rhyssa and Auric. They're explorers and galactic cartographers, so Lina knows how to think fast in the unsafe scenarios she and her brother often find themselves in. Milo relies on Lina to fix things (in a literal sense, she's talented with machines), and she always does. Lina's desire to find and rescue their parents lead her and Milo to the underground Rebels Ephraim and Mira Bridger on Lothal.

# Luminara Unduli

*"Gentlemen, if you are quite finished, we have a battle to begin."*

⟟⌁⍀⟟⋔⌰⌰⋔⌿⌰⌿

Could you remain calm if you were held captive by zombies and about to be forcibly infected by brain worms? Mirialan Jedi Master Luminara Unduli is known for keeping a level head in the most trying of scenarios—even when confronted with parasites during a mission on Geonosis. She's also known for playing by the rules, and she passes her disciplined perspective to her Padawan Barriss Offee, who unfortunately will find the Jedi falling short of her own principled standards with deadly consequences.

First seen in *Attack of the Clones*, Luminara leads many missions for the Army of the Republic in *Star Wars: The Clone Wars*. Her aptitude for strategic planning and combat with or without a lightsaber makes her a valuable general. Stationed on the Wookiee homeworld of Kashyyyk upon the issue of Order 66, she escapes slaughter but is captured by the Empire, who use her to lay a trap for the remaining Jedi.

# Lyra Erso

*"Trust the Force."*

ᔑᐯᔔᖽ ᐯᓰᘔᔑᐸ

Facing grave danger with the arrival of Imperial forces, Lyra urges her daughter Jyn to follow a plan for her own safety, and to put trust in the Force. It's not an easy sentiment for someone to pass on when they've been through what Lyra Erso has. But despite the many hardships she's encountered, her belief stays strong. Even before dying at the hands of Orson Krennic's death troopers in *Rogue One*, Lyra left her daughter with a message of hope and a kyber crystal pendant. Strong-willed and sharp enough to see through the Empire's manipulations of her husband Galen, Lyra risks everything to keep her family safe—including setting up a contingency plan with her friend Saw Gerrera, who comes to Lah'mu to evacuate Jyn.

Before the events of *Rogue One*, Lyra worked as a geologist who studies crystals. Her work with natural environments on different worlds around the galaxy speaks to her on a spiritual level as well as a scientific one, leading her to study the Force and the ways of the Jedi Order. Lyra finds a unique balance between the scientific and the spiritual; it helps her attain clarity about the Empire's intentions.

# Mama the Hutt

*"Should have figured, after all these years of never callin', you'd show up at dinner time."*

⌐⌐⌐⌐ ⌐⌐⌐ ⌐⌐⌐⌐

Many of us are guilty of not staying in touch with our family. Mama the Hutt knows what it's like to be ignored and forgotten. We first visit her home in the swamps of Nal Hutta when her son Ziro the Hutt crawls to her doorstep begging for a favor in *The Clone Wars*. Typical. She'd been living alone for years, getting by with the help of hovering housekeeper droids. Mama, the grandmother of Jabba the Hutt, is none too pleased with her deadbeat son, but she acts in magnanimous fashion anyway and helps him. It's what mothers do.

Visitors only come to Mama the Hutt's home on rare occasions, but the over a thousand-year-old matriarch stays mindful of her appearance. She wears a stylish stack of small black creatures called Sha'rellian toops atop her head.

# Maz Kanata

*"Hope is not lost today. It is found."*

ᒷᔑᓵ ᒲᔑ⼞ᔑᖋᔑ

*All are welcome. (No fighting.)* Everyone who arrives at Maz Kanata's castle—smuggler, bounty hunter, and traveler alike—sees and is expected to abide by this sign upon entering. But while this is her establishment's only rule, Maz herself is a strong fighter, and is ready to demonstrate this skill when the need arises. A pirate queen and legend revealed in *The Force Awakens*, Maz is open to the galaxy around her and the beings who call it home—unless those beings cause trouble. She demonstrates what it's like to be kind and welcoming while maintaining a zero-tolerance policy for anyone jeopardizing what she has built. It's a precarious balance, but it's one she's been able to maintain for more than a thousand years.

Though small in stature, Maz is tough. She's been injured sixty-seven times, and twenty-two of the injuries were life-threatening. She has a commanding presence. Inspired by *The Force Awakens* director J.J. Abrams and production designer Rick Carter's English teacher, Rose Gilbert, Maz was almost brought to life as a puppet or animatronic. But Abrams soon realized they should employ a motion capture process to create the pirate queen, both because they didn't find a puppet design early enough, and they thought an animatronic might limit what the character could do. So, they used computer graphics to enhance the creature qualities of the character, but based her expressive movements in the performance of actress

Lupita Nyong'o. "The performance was all Lupita," said Abrams. "She was there on set, and we did capture sessions afterwards as well, and I can't say enough about working with her."

Nyong'o found the idea of inhabiting the role in this way appealing. "What attracted me [to the role] was, first of all, the opportunity to play a motion capture character. I thought that gave me a unique experience, where I got to play a character that wasn't limited by my physical circumstances." But it wasn't easy. "The first time I came onto set in that suit, it was the most alienating thing in the world. Because there are lights shining on my face, everyone is drawn to look at me. I was fighting nerves, butterflies, in my stomach, and feeling very self-conscious. I was still trying to figure out how to be this completely different person in this suit, and to have an understanding of my physicality and the space around me. It was bizarre."

It took more than Nyong'o to bring Maz to the screen. Actress Arti Shah also worked with Nyong'o as a motion capture double for Maz. "I was very lucky to have met Lupita," said Shah. "She was such a pleasure to work with. She would tell me how she wanted Maz to come across, but also ask my perspective with regards to Maz's height, and how quickly she would walk. As a small person, I tend to take small but quick steps."

Maz's castle on the planet Takodana is the place to go for loans, repairs, games of chance, hideout, or to start your smuggling career. She will occasionally leave home in one of her starships to see firsthand what's going on, taking the pulse of the galaxy as a way to anticipate trouble and maintain her own order. Maz is versatile; she's comfortable as a pilot, operating a jet-pack, and using knitting needles. She has seen much in her long life, including the Galactic Civil War and the rise and fall of the Empire, and warns about the shadow of the First Order spreading. She understands them as part of a continuum and as a threat to be opposed, but this is a fight she'll conduct in her own way.

Maz cares about her business, but she's not selfish, and is generous with her time and connections. She's forged alliances with everyone from industrious transporters to master codebreakers.

"Being a hero is not about success or failure, being a hero means stepping forward, no matter the outcome."

—Maz Kanata

It's an aspect Nyong'o likes: "Maz, herself, I was attracted to the heart of her." In *Forces of Destiny*, in which Maz is the host and keeper of the stories being told in the animated shorts, we see her help Leia acquire her Boushh disguise, used in the mission to rescue Han from Jabba's palace. Decades later, when Han arrives on her doorstep with Finn and Rey looking for assistance in *The Force Awakens*, she gives them honest advice (and asks teasingly about her "boyfriend," Chewbacca). She tells Han to stop avoiding Leia, explains to Finn why he should fight against the evil of the First Order, and encourages Rey to use the Force when she finds Anakin and Luke Skywalker's lightsaber in one of Maz's castle storage rooms: "The belonging you seek is not behind you. It is ahead. I am no Jedi, but I know the Force. It moves through and surrounds every living thing. Close your eyes. Feel it. The light. It's always been there. It will guide you."

# Mira Bridger

*"Without hope, we have nothing."*

ᒧᓓᔐ ᔕᔓᓓᒪ ᐁᓓᔐ

To oppose the Galactic Empire is to put your life and the lives of those you care about on the line. Mira Bridger knows the risks of taking a stand, but the possible consequences don't stop her from speaking out against the Empire when they occupy her homeworld of Lothal. She first appears in *Star Wars Rebels* in a picture found by her son Ezra. It's a picture and not an in person meeting because Mira and her husband Ephraim are in an Imperial prison, sentenced for treason.

Courageous and dedicated to helping Lothal's citizens, Mira broadcasts underground messages to speak the truth about the Empire. Her words spark the fire of revolution; a revolution that continues long after her imprisonment. While Ezra carries on their work, Mira and Ephraim are inspired to organize a prison break, and though they perish in the effort, they do so as they lived: fighting for others.

# Mon Mothma

*"I have no fear as I take new action.
For I am not alone."*

ᒋᐤᑎ ᒋᐤᐱᘿᒪᐸ

When Mon Mothma first appears in *Return of the Jedi*, she is the portrait of poise. She delivers both good and bad news at the Rebel briefing for the attack on the second Death Star, and does so with a quiet but commanding power. Her very presence emanates serenity under stress. As the second high-ranking female character fans see in the Rebel Alliance in the original trilogy, she makes an impression. But her appearance before the Battle of Endor is just a small part of her story.

Mon Mothma, a native of Chandrila, is one of the most pivotal characters in the *Star Wars* saga. A co-founder of the Rebel Alliance and a chancellor of the New Republic, she's a revolutionary who's put everything into making the galaxy a peaceful, prosperous place since the days of the Clone Wars. Her politics, the kind that involve weathering near-constant galactic conflict, take a heavy toll. "Yes. It is hard," she says. "But we persevere. Like the Rebel Alliance before us, like the New Republic now. We persevere."

To the joy of fans who wanted more of Mon Mothma after her brief scene in *Return of the Jedi*, her importance has come to light in stories spanning the timeline. *Star Wars: The Clone Wars* shows us the seeds of Rebellion are planted years before Emperor Palpatine makes his power grab. Mon Mothma's there from the beginning, convening with senators like Padmé Amidala and Bail Organa to

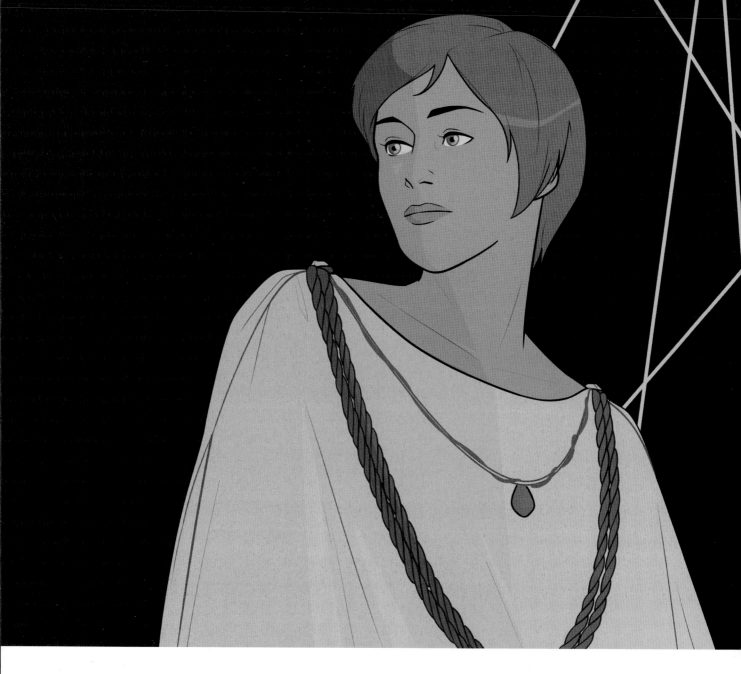

"We will not rest until we bring an end to the Empire, until we restore our Republic! Are you with me?"

—Mon Mothma

discuss how to resolve the struggle between the Separatists and the Galactic Republic. After that war ends and the true nature of the Empire starts coming to light, Mon and Bail meet in secret with other concerned parties. These rendezvous lead to the formation of insurgent groups around the galaxy.

The breaking point comes in *Star Wars Rebels*. After learning about the slaughter of peaceful protesters on the planet Ghorman, Mon speaks out against Emperor Palpatine in public, knowing she'll be branded a traitor. She demonstrates that there's a time for valiant action beyond politics. This is, in effect, the official beginning of the Rebel Alliance. She gathers the scattered cells with an emotional speech, "For too long I have watched the heavy hand of the Empire strangle our liberties, stifling our freedoms in the name of ensuring our safety. No longer! Despite Imperial threats, despite the Emperor himself, I have no fear as I take new action. For I am not alone. Beginning today we stand together as allies."

Mon Mothma is voiced by Genevieve O'Reilly in *Rebels*, the same actress who portrays her in deleted scenes from *Revenge of the Sith* and in *Rogue One*. She studied Caroline Blakiston's original performance in *Return of the Jedi* to mimic how Blakiston carries herself and how she speaks. O'Reilly admires the character: "She really shows the traits of a true leader in very difficult, very heightened, dangerous times. I think by her nature she's a genuine humanitarian. She has a strong moral compass. She's also a critical thinker and she is a considered decision maker. We meet her at those moments where there is a crux, a fork in the road, a genuine point that requires her leadership. That's what's really interesting, to see that early leadership and where it grew from."

After Emperor Palpatine's death, Mon knows the threat of the Empire isn't over just because its head has been removed. First chancellor of the reestablished Galactic Senate, she guides the budding government through the transition period. She's instrumental in bringing the New Republic's full force to the Battle of Jakku, which leads to the signing of the Galactic Concordance and official surrender of the Empire.

# Mother Talzin

*"Where one sees failure, others see opportunity."*

ᘓᐤᘦᘓᗐᒐ ᘦᛕᘦᘑᕊᘓ

Mother Talzin once said, "I am a simple witch." That is not exactly true. The leader of the Nightsisters of Dathomir coven, Talzin employs supernatural tactics to advance her shrewd plans, and wields enormous dark magick powers again and again in *Star Wars: The Clone Wars*, shaping green mystical energy into weapons, and at one point later bringing her son Darth Maul back from the edge of madness. Above anything and anyone else, she longs to be the most powerful being in the galaxy.

Her talents are so impressive that Darth Sidious makes a special trip to Dathomir, promising to offer the wisdom and secrets of the dark side, but kidnapping young Maul to serve as his apprentice instead. As a leader, Talzin is as fiercely protective of her clan as she is loyal to her son, and she sees what's called for is revenge against the Sith, Sidious, and his next apprentice, Count Dooku. In this she'll find common cause with Asajj Ventress, a Nightsister taken from them as an infant in exchange for the clan's safety, who has returned with her own grudge against the Sith.

Mother Talzin's look dates back to *The Phantom Menace* and artist Iain McCaig's concept for a female Sith, unused in the prequel film trilogy but finding a home in *The Clone Wars*. She's voiced by Barbara Goodson, who drew upon Maria Ouspenskaya's performance from 1941's *The Wolf Man* for inspiration for the witch's voice, and enjoys the echo effect used for Talzin's dialogue: "If I'm a person who's been around for—I'm basically immortal, right? I'm channeling ancient energies, so they're all in me."

# Norra Wexley

*"My job isn't fighting this war anymore.
My job is you."*

ᴎᴀⵎⵎⰓ ⵑᴍᴀⵎⴼᴍ

Spurred to join the fight against the Empire after her husband is captured by Imperials, Norra Wexley puts her twelve-year-old son Temmin "Snap" Wexley in her sisters' care on their homeworld of Akiva and devotes herself to the cause of the Rebellion. At first serving as a freighter pilot, she's enlisted in the Battle of Endor to fly a Y-wing fighter/bomber in the assault on the second Death Star, and plays a key role in its destruction, for which she is decorated. In the *Aftermath* trilogy of novels, following events of *Return of the Jedi* and preceding *The Force Awakens*, we see Norra torn between her parental duties to her son and her military duties to the galaxy, leading missions to hunt down the remnants of the Empire, including Imperial Grand Admiral Rae Sloane. Her headstrong attitude means she sometimes (often) leaps into conflict without a fully considered plan, but it can also lead her to important discoveries, such as finding the remnants of the Imperial fleet and setting in motion the Battle of Jakku and the downfall of the Empire.

# Numa

Freedom fighter on Ryloth who's been
part of conflict her entire life.

ᗯᑌᗰᗩ

Numa's life is defined from an early age by her struggle for survival. Orphaned as a child during the Separatist invasion of her homeworld of Ryloth, the young Twi'lek is cannily able to avoid the droid forces by hiding in her town's underground tunnel network. In *Star Wars: The Clone Wars*, we see her courageously help Obi-Wan Kenobi and the clone troopers of the Republic stop the invading army, in the process inspiring her fellow captive Twi'leks and making an emotional connection with several of the clones.

Numa's already tough core strengthens as she becomes an adult. Embroiled in the constant conflict on her planet and determined to take action, Numa joins Cham Syndulla's (father of Hera Syndulla) Free Ryloth movement and becomes one of the group's finest warriors. In standing against the Galactic Empire, Numa and the movement find common cause with Rebel cells such as the Spectres, and in *Star Wars Rebels* we see them work together to carry on the fight.

# Oola

Captive performer for Jabba the Hutt whose fate might have been different.

◻◻◻⤙K

In the shifting cast of characters who inhabit Jabba the Hutt's palace, all manner of bounty hunters, smugglers, and performers gather in the dark corners of the creepy crime lord's abode—some present by choice, and some without the freedom to decide. The Twi'lek dancer Oola falls into the latter category. She appears in *Return of the Jedi* as the second ever Twi'lek to be featured in the galaxy. Oola's lekku, or head-tails, were designed to respond to actress Femi Taylor's gestures and movements; to that end, they were made with foam latex to be as lightweight as possible. They were blended into Oola's green skin makeup, which took four hours to apply.

Oola's story is not a joyful one. Kidnapped by Jabba's majordomo Bib Fortuna, Oola trains in the art of exotic dancing. She's forced to perform for Jabba, but she does so with reluctance and often defies his orders. We see her doing so on-screen for the last time, with fatal results. According to Taylor, things might have been different: a sequence had been considered in which Oola escapes her fate and Jabba's palace, but was cut, apparently due to budget restrictions.

# Padmé Amidala

*"There is always a choice!
To live in fear is no life at all."*

᚟ᚷᚖ ᚲᚵᚔᚴᚲ ᚾᚲ

One of the galaxy's most optimistic and resilient characters, Padmé Amidala Naberrie pours her faith and belief into the people and the government around her, even when they don't behave the way she wishes they would. Her devotion sustains her through a lifetime of public service. She becomes an Apprentice Legislator when she's eight years old, is elected Queen of Naboo at the age of fourteen, and later serves as a senator representing her home planet. Padmé gives her all to the galaxy.

Our introduction to Padmé in *The Phantom Menace* is as Queen Amidala, and although young, she is not to be underestimated. The Trade Federation can't trick or intimidate her into signing documents to make their blockade of Naboo legal, and when the Republic refuses to come to Naboo's aid, Padmé calls them out: "I was not elected to watch my people suffer and die while you discuss this invasion in a committee!" To protect Naboo, she breaks down barriers by enlisting the native Gungans as allies against the invading Trade Federation—a partnership no one before her had considered. The strategy works.

Her political prowess and bridge-building are important, and show strength of character more diverse than the obvious heroics of lightsaber combat or being able to pilot a starship through battle.

"I will not condone a course of action that will lead us to war."

—Padmé Amidala

Though she's an excellent shot with a blaster, Padmé's specialties lie in speaking and thinking clearly about justice, and in serving and defending this ideal.

The nature of Padmé's career creates a duality of sorts we don't see many other characters navigate. As the Queen of Naboo, she wears elaborate gowns and makeup that obscures her face. The mask-like cosmetics are helpful when one of Padmé's loyal handmaidens steps in to disguise herself as her decoy, but it also delineates her role in office. In full queen attire, she also speaks in a deeper tone and carries herself in a more regal manner. It suggests the way in which she understands the balance and distinction between her personal and professional lives, an aspect also evident when she marries Anakin Skywalker in secret in *Attack of the Clones*.

Padmé's wardrobe reflects the way she stands in two worlds. When she's alone with Anakin, the lines of her costumes are softer. When she's sitting as queen or serving in the senate, her ensembles are heavier and more formal. She wears the weight of office. Costume designer Trisha Biggar imagined more than thirty costumes for Padmé in the prequels at the behest of George Lucas. His scripts expanded the fashion of the galaxy to show more opulent looks than the ones featured in the original trilogy. One of the most complex of Padmé's gowns is the red throne room dress she dons as Queen of Naboo. The Chinese Imperial court-influenced garment took almost eight weeks to finish. And that's just *one* of her outfits.

After completing two terms as a beloved queen, Padmé accepts an appointment to the Galactic Senate. As the Separatist Alliance forms, the Senate debates the formation of a military, and we see Padmé strongly oppose this move. The position nearly gets her killed—Zam Wesell tries to assassinate her the night before the vote—but Padmé is more concerned about the fate the galaxy will suffer in wartime than for her personal safety. Once the Clone Wars begin, she fights against the creation of additional soldiers. In *Star Wars: The Clone Wars*, she pleads with the Republic to use funds to aid its citizens instead of creating five million more clones. "My people, your people, all of our people. This war is meant to save them from suffering. Not increase it. It is our duty and our responsibility to preserve the lives of those around us by defeating this bill."

In *The Clone Wars* we also see Padmé head into the field to gather information herself, sometimes on her own initiative, and sometimes at the request of the Jedi. Her trips are of a diplomatic nature, but at times she's required to enter into, as she calls it, "aggressive negotiations." In one case, as she prepares to embark on a risky offworld mission to determine a fellow senator's true motives, Anakin tries to tell Padmé she's not allowed to go. She will have none of it: "You're not going to let me? It's not your decision to make. It's mine."

In her role as a diplomat, she sees the importance of maintaining a pragmatic, clear-eyed perspective when the galaxy and the players around her are in a heightened, agitated state. Padmé passes on a more complete picture of the war between the Separatists and the Republic to Ahsoka Tano, and opens the Padawan's eyes to the deeper currents of the conflict—nuance Anakin doesn't see, since he really only knows the Republic's side. She leads by example, negotiating with the likes of Duchess Satine Kryze, ruler of the planet Mandalore, and Separatist Senator Mina Bonteri. Padmé is willing to set partisanship aside, if it means coming to an accord that ends the war.

Voice actress Catherine Taber sees Padmé as a role model, and cites the character's open perspective as a quality she admires. "She has taught me about compassion. Despite her elite history as both a queen and a politician, she is able to cross all kinds of boundaries that often isolate us from one another, maintaining meaningful relationships with people from all different walks of life and opposing views. She seeks out commonalities as opposed to differences. I admire that tremendously."

Padmé puts her career on the line for the sake of the galaxy, too. Some senators believe the narrative then Supreme Chancellor Palpatine weaves throughout the war, even as he begins to twist it against the Jedi. Padmé doesn't suspect Palpatine is actually a dangerous Sith Lord, but she knows something is wrong, and shares her concerns with a small group of politicians, includ-

"*Far too often, we forget that our most important allies are not always the most powerful.*"

—Padmé Amidala

ing Bail Organa and Mon Mothma. Her goal here, as always, is to try to preserve peace in the Republic. As the Clone Wars spiral into chaos, and Palpatine names himself as Emperor of the new Galactic Empire, most of the Senate cheers, but not Padmé. Standing with Bail, she observes, "This is how liberty dies, with thunderous applause." Bail and Mon later become primary architects in the Rebellion against this new corrupt and evil Empire.

Padmé Amidala's legacy is much more than the children she gives birth to, Luke Skywalker and Leia Organa. Her final words encapsulate her life. Still seeing the possibility for light within Anakin, she tells Obi-Wan, "There is good in him." She believes in others, and in the galaxy, to the very end.

# Padmé's Handmaidens

Attendants to the Queen and
more than meets the eye.

ᑕᖇ�ᗰ ᗱᑲᗹᕼᑲᔼᐁᐃᑲᗱ

The role of a Naboo Royal Handmaiden is, by design, much deeper than appearance suggests. At the most basic level, they assist with everyday tasks, including choosing gowns and styling hair. But they're also advisers, confidantes and bodyguards, trained in deception, defense, and strength in service to their queen.

In *The Phantom Menace* and *Attack of the Clones*, we meet Padmé Amidala's retinue, particularly Sabé, Cordé, and Dormé. In joining the handmaidens, each has made a commitment in full knowledge of the risk and responsibility involved. Beyond learning marksmanship and melee combat, they study how to communicate through subtle gestures and how to mimic the queen. Their duties include stepping in as decoys for any situation in which the queen may be at risk; for that reason, they must also somewhat resemble the woman they serve. Sabé poses as the queen when the Trade Federation invades Naboo, and Cordé impersonates her before the Military Creation Act vote and dies in her service. Dormé stays by Padmé's side during her time in the senate as an aide who manages her affairs.

The concept of handmaidens as decoys goes all the way back to George Lucas's rough draft of *Star Wars*. Princess Leia Organa had two handmaidens, and in order to keep her out of the Empire's hands, the handmaiden who most resembled her took her place. The idea found new life decades later with the Naboo Royal Handmaidens.

# Paige Tico

*"The Resistance is built on belief."*

ᴄᴋ1ᴜᴠ1 ↓1ɴᴏ

Paige Tico had just a few moments of screen time in *The Last Jedi*, but she has an immeasurable impact on the story and on the viewer. In a heart-pounding sequence when she understands that dropping her ship's proton bombs on the First Order Dreadnought during the evacuation of D'Qar is down to her and her alone, she uses every ounce of determination and strength to get to and press the button on a remote, releasing the weapons. Paige's actions encapsulate the spirit of the Resistance. Bravery, focus, heart—she embodies those qualities as she closes her eyes, grasps her medallion, and sacrifices herself.

Paige wears one half of this medallion, and her sister Rose wears the other. Made from material found on their homeworld of Hays Minor, it's a gift from their parents. Paige, or as Rose sometimes calls her, Pae-Pae, is the older sibling, and fiercely protective of Rose. She's the first one to comfort Rose, but is also the first to push her to use her true talents and ingenuity.

After witnessing the way the First Order brutalizes her home and other worlds in her star system, Paige joins the Resistance. She serves as a gunner aboard the *Cobalt Hammer*, and is a skilled pilot, enamored with flying since she sat on her mom's lap in the cockpit of an oredigger. She honors her parents and sister by never giving up.

# Phasma

*"The First Order is not the Empire. We are purer. We have been through the crucible and emerged stronger."*

ᘁᗐᛕᘉᘊᛕ

Captain Phasma marches into the *Star Wars* galaxy with authority, in a suit of dazzling chromium armor. As the first female villain in a leading role in a *Star Wars* movie, she commands attention, and was the subject of intense speculation in the months leading into *The Force Awakens*. A captain in the First Order, she's responsible for shaping the stormtroopers into model, malleable soldiers who will obey every order. Phasma may follow the commands of her superiors in the First Order, but make no mistake: everything she does, she does for herself.

The *Phasma* novel reveals the character's origins on the planet Parnassos. Born into a primitive clan in a world devastated by a nuclear reaction, Phasma arranges the deaths of her clan and even her own parents in order to ensure her own survival. Utterly ruthless, she proclaims herself the greatest warrior on the planet. As Resistance spy Vi Moradi tells a member of the First Order, "No one will go as far as she will to survive." *Phasma* author Delilah Dawson describes the character as having "zero doubts about exactly who she is and what she's willing to do, and there's something so seductive about that kind of confidence."

Her Phasma-first attitude helps her earn a place within the First Order. When Brendol Hux's ship crashes on Parnassos, Phasma

seizes the opportunity to join him and the First Order and escape her home planet. She's confident, and knows how to sell herself. Actress Gwendoline Christie projects these attributes in her performance as the first female stormtrooper on the screen: "It's exciting that something as iconic as *Star Wars* has embraced the future and has embraced the world's need for gender balance and female empowerment. I hope it inspires generations of women everywhere to go forward."

Phasma's chromium-coated armor gives her an air of mystery, something Phasma herself is well aware of. The material has been salvaged from a yacht once owned by Emperor Palpatine. Behind the scenes, costume designer Michael Kaplan originally came up with the silver armor look for Kylo Ren. It didn't work for his character in the end, but after Lucasfilm president Kathleen Kennedy complimented the concept art, it became Phasma's. That armor, which they only had five days to make, inspired the character's name. The design reminded *The Force Awakens* director J.J. Abrams of the 1979 horror film *Phantasm*.

"The costume is absolutely sensational," says Christie. "It is restrictive, but I think it gives us an insight into Captain Phasma. This is a woman who is wearing armor, but her femininity is still displayed. She doesn't try to hide it; it only empowers her further. The costume takes around forty-five minutes to put on. It certainly makes me stand up straight." She also likes that Phasma doesn't remove her helmet: "I thought it was a really interesting opportunity to play a female character, where we formed an opinion of her based on her actions, rather than the way she has been made flesh."

We don't even see a glimpse of Phasma's face until *The Last Jedi* when she's fighting Finn, her former trooper FN-2187, who left the First Order to join the Resistance. The helmet was re-chromed for the film to show less distress, but it also takes a significant hit in the battle. Director Rian Johnson told Kaplan he wanted the helmet to have an open split, but Kaplan went for something more subtle instead: "I put aluminum foil in the big gash in the helmet and closed it up. You just saw this eye. It was beautiful, and he really liked that. She has piercing blue eyes, too, which is unexpected."

> "You never know a soldier's true worth until they've stood on the battlefield, faced with death."
>
> —Phasma

Held aloft as a model First Order soldier, Phasma, in her armor, shines in propaganda posters. She teaches stormtroopers to place their loyalties to the First Order, not each other, but this is not a code she follows herself. In *The Force Awakens*, Phasma takes down Starkiller Base's shields under threat from Finn, which contributes to the destruction of the planet. But facing charges of treason, we see her in Marvel's *Captain Phasma* comic working the system and eliminating anyone who learns her secrets—a one-woman task force and murderous clean-up squad. Phasma tells a rival, "I fought for everything that I have, every bit of what I am."

After Finn threatened her in *The Force Awakens*, fans couldn't wait to see Phasma face him again in *The Last Jedi*. She finds the First Order traitor aboard Supreme Leader Snoke's ship, *Supremacy*, and is eager to serve a painful form of justice to FN-2187. No one she commands knows what happened on Starkiller, and she doesn't reveal her hand. She doesn't owe anyone explanations; she simply commands First Order stormtrooper executioners to make Finn's final moments hurt.

# Qi'ra

*"Everyone has secrets. If I told you mine,
I'd just have to go find new ones."*

⊏1'7⊧

From wearing ragged clothes reeking of the Corellian sewers she grew up in to sporting tailored designer gowns aboard an opulent yacht, from dismal circumstance to opportunity won by determination, wit, and skill, Qi'ra charts a remarkable and ambitious path for herself. Committed to rising above her station, Qi'ra climbs the ranks of the criminal organization Crimson Dawn under the gangster Dryden Vos to become his most trusted strategist and adviser, positioning herself as an excellent observer and expert manipulator. She knows when to flatter, when to cajole, and when to change the topic—maybe with violence. She's interested in money and influence, but what matters most is survival.

Qi'ra's a femme fatale unlike other heroines in the *Star Wars* films. Introduced in *Solo: A Star Wars Story*, Qi'ra relies on intelligence, charisma, and lies to advance her ultimate goal—to be free of people chasing her. Her appreciation for finer things is rooted in her hard knock youth. As a scrumrat for the White Worm gang alongside Han, she lives in the sewer, surviving on unsavory rations doled out by the gang's leader, Lady Proxima. It's as dire as it sounds: starved for comforts, Qi'ra imagines stealing throw pillows from a hotel lobby, just to have something nice. But in her time as one of Proxima's scrumrats, Qi'ra learns tactics that will serve her in the future, not the least of which is perfecting the art of keeping her

"I think it's impractical to make a big decision based on a feeling."

—Qi'ra

face emotionless in situations when displaying her feelings could mean losing leverage.

To earn more freedom, and maybe the occasional piece of fruit, Qi'ra takes her service to Proxima seriously, hoping to be promoted to Head Girl. In the novel *Most Wanted*, she competes with Han for advancement, but their rivalry leads to an alliance. Qi'ra's calculated planning ensures their survival, as they're on the run from dangerous arms dealers again and again. She isn't able to escape Corellia with Han, but she finds her own way. When we see her next, she's on Dryden Vos's star yacht, having left behind the White Worms to join Crimson Dawn. It's absolutely a step up, and even luxurious, in a way, but Qi'ra knows it has not come without a cost. When Han asks how she got out of Corellia, out of a life serving Proxima, Qi'ra tells him she didn't—she's just serving a different kind of master.

Vos keeps Qi'ra close, benefiting from her observations of the environment around her; Qi'ra excels at assessing what's happening, and finding escape routes (as a scrumrat, she once escaped a desperate situation by tricking her opponents into breaking a window, creating a distraction). Her time with Proxima, who loves flattery, teaches Qi'ra what to say to deflect or please, which is useful in placating Vos and handling his volatile nature. And as part of the underworld for all of her life, she understands the need to be able to take care of herself in a fight; she's good with a blaster, and has trained in Teräs Käsi, a hand-to-hand combat discipline.

Actress Emilia Clarke notes Qi'ra's guarded nature and how it's hard to be sure of the character's motives. "There is a thing throughout the [Han and Qi'ra] relationship you just can't put your finger on. And that's Qi'ra. Every time you think you have got her number you realize you haven't at all. Which is really hard to play." And she acknowledges not all that glitters is gold, saying, "Well, if you have got a really glamorous lady in a really sordid environment you kind of know that maybe the glamour is hiding a few rough roads."

Qi'ra's exact trajectory into Crimson Dawn isn't detailed, but it's hinted at that she's more than paid her dues to escape Proxima's tentacled grasp. Whatever her route, she looks at home on Vos's decadent business-meets-pleasure yacht. Qi'ra's presence is such that she's the shining light of any room she's in, and uses that magnetism to her advantage. Vos's guests and employees represent a variety of alien creature types, and Qi'ra was almost one of those species. Early ideation for *Solo* envisioned Kura— later to be called Qi'ra, a riff on the name Kira, which was used for Rey in early drafts of *The Force Awakens*—as a humanoid alien. But after a number of concepts and sketches, it was decided the character would best be served by a performance uninhibited by prosthetics.

And Clarke's range is apparent when Qi'ra encounters Han, after years apart. Maybe joining Crimson Dawn isn't the life Qi'ra would have chosen for herself, but she's taken stock of what the gang gives her and made a life and built a reputation. When Qi'ra's appointed to the crew and tasked with stealing unrefined coaxium by Vos, it's because of her carefully cultivated connections that they're able to acquire a speedy ship. When she sees Han, she comments on being trapped, but in a matter-of-fact sort of way. She relishes having power and being able to get what she wants. Qi'ra knows she could handle business better, and certainly more calmly, than Vos. So, when she sees a chance for promotion, she takes it.

Killing Vos grants her control, eliminating the most controlling individual in her life. With Vos and his time-wasting, rash decisions out of the way, Qi'ra has cleared a path for herself to rise within Crimson Dawn. This act of self-determination is why her betrayal of Han isn't sad, not really. In that moment when she takes command of Vos's ship and contacts Maul, Qi'ra, who has been shuffled around by the galaxy to some degree all her life, claims agency. She finally chooses her own direction.

"Somebody falls, you keep running.
It's how you stay alive."

—Qi'ra

# R2-KT

The droid with the heart of gold.

フヨ⁻コ↓

Among the many exceptional droids in the galaxy, R2-KT is something special. The pink astromech was inspired by a real-life creation designed by the R2-D2 Builders Club. They constructed R2-KT for Katie Johnson, a young girl diagnosed with terminal brain cancer who wished she had a droid to watch over her, just as R2-D2 watches over Padmé Amidala in *Attack of the Clones*. Since Katie loved the color pink, the builders made a special pastel astromech for her. R2-KT stayed by Katie's side through her last days.

R2-KT joins the galaxy on-screen in the animated feature *Star Wars: The Clone Wars* as one of the droids serving the 501st Legion—fitting, because Katie's father Albin is the founder of the 501st Legion fan group. After loyally serving the Republic and characters such as Anakin Skywalker during the Clone Wars, R2-KT continues to serve galactic good as part of the Resistance, and can be spotted in *The Force Awakens*.

# Rae Sloane

*"If you ever cross me, I will visit this same violence upon you a hundredfold."*

7ꓘ∇Ɩ ⅃⅃Ɔꓘ∧∇Ɩ

Rae Sloane is a formidable character in the story of the Empire, with roots stretching from before the original trilogy—she was introduced in the novel *A New Dawn*—to events following *Return of the Jedi*. Born on the industrial, shipyard-rich planet of Ganthel, Rae witnesses the Empire put an end to criminal operations on her homeworld, and so views them as a positive influence on the galaxy. After graduating from the Imperial naval academy, she blazes quite a trail, gaining her first captaincy by the age of thirty and ultimately rising through the ranks to become Grand Admiral. She even foils an assassination attempt against Darth Vader and the Emperor by her own commandant while serving as a lieutenant. Rae is committed to what she perceives as the Empire's values, and as the highest-ranked surviving officer after the Battle of Endor, we see her work tirelessly to keep the Imperial military from extinction in the *Aftermath* novels.

Following the death of the Emperor, Rae sees the Empire falling short of her own ideals under the influence of Fleet Admiral Gallius Rax. Fueled by her lifelong dedication, she pushes back against his leadership, and executes him during the Battle of Jakku, leading the remnants of the Empire into the Unknown Regions, determined to rebuild. She proclaims, "It's time to start over. That is our first order. To begin again. And to get it right, this time."

*Aftermath* trilogy author Chuck Wendig says Rae Sloane was one of his favorite characters to write because we see the Empire through her eyes. "She has an ethos and, on paper, it's ostensibly a positive one even if the Empire she serves is ultimately autocratic and malevolent. Her motivations are human and, at least to me, understandable even as they remain something to condemn."

# Rey

*"I think I can handle myself."*

"I know how to run without you holding my hand." The central character in the film trilogy beginning with *The Force Awakens*, Rey arrives in the tradition of heroes such as Leia Organa and Padmé Amidala—outspoken, independent, and self-sufficient—but she is also uniquely important to the saga and to the fans. Rey, a young woman from the dusty, nothing-ever-happens-here planet of Jakku, receives the call to adventure that changes her life and alters the fandom landscape. Few moments in *Star Wars* are as powerful as Anakin and Luke Skywalker's lightsaber flying out of a snowbank and into Rey's outstretched hand.

Reaction to Rey joining the *Star Wars* galaxy was immediate and passionate. She inspires creative expressions throughout fandom: art, essays, replicas of her distinctive triple bun hairstyle, and costumes at conventions and fan gatherings everywhere. She's a hero without arrogance, a character without all the answers—who wouldn't want to be like her?

Daisy Ridley was unsure, and a little worried, about what fans would think of Rey. Before *The Force Awakens* was released, she said, "I realized what this film might be to people. I hope that people will love it. I think they will. I feel like I'm working with my film family. Every day is fun. I haven't had one day where I didn't enjoy it. There

are moments when I think how many people love *Star Wars*, and it's scary trying to fit into that world that people know so well and love so much. It's nerve-wracking thinking about what Rey might represent to these people and whether they'll like her or not."

Rey would go through a hero's journey behind the scenes, too. Early stages depict her working in a used spaceship lot, longing to leave her world behind—unlike Rey in the film, who stays put awaiting the return of her family. Even in initial drafts, Kira is a scavenger with a speeder she makes herself, but little else remains of the original direction. Subsequent drafts of the script shape Kira into Rey, and a hero is born.

Rey grows up alone on Jakku, an unforgiving planet that can wring dry those who call it home. Left by her parents as a young girl, Rey doesn't receive much help from anyone. She quickly learns the ins-and-outs of survival: not just how to search the wreckage from the Battle of Jakku for profitable parts, but also how to protect herself from the dangers of the desert and fellow scavengers. Rey teaches herself how to fight with a staff. She looks at each item she finds from the perspective of possibility, whether turning lenses from a stormtrooper helmet into goggles, or uncovering a fallen AT-AT walker to make it her home.

Rey is kind, and she's optimistic, even when trapped in a situation that would turn most people cynical and cold, let down and betrayed by others time and again. She demonstrates this kindness when she lets the lost droid BB-8 follow her home in *The Force Awakens*, rather than sell him for more food than she's ever seen; and again when she feeds a fearsome Nightwatcher worm precious salvaged material so it doesn't starve in *Forces of Destiny*; and most importantly when she helps Finn, a complete stranger, get away from the First Order following his desertion by taking him offworld.

By trusting Finn and leaving the dust of Jakku behind, Rey opens a door to a life she couldn't have imagined. She's dreamed of it; the Force showed her Luke's island while she slept, but how often do visions become reality? She meets the legendary smuggler Han Solo. She sees a planet with more green than she thought existed. Her wonder is our wonder. We see the galaxy through her earnest eyes, and it's like experiencing it for the first time. This makes Rey's discovery of her Force abilities all the more powerful.

The Force inside of Rey awakens when she first touches the lightsaber that once belonged to the Skywalkers. It calls to her while she's on Takodana. Maz Kanata tries to help Rey process what's happened, but scared of the intensity of the Force vision, Rey runs. She doesn't see herself as anything special, so of course she doesn't immediately embrace her powers. Her abilities awaken powerfully after she's captured by Kylo Ren, and his reaction to her strength emboldens her to test her newfound skills. The resolve we see on Jakku returns as she escapes and then confronts Kylo Ren head-on.

Their lightsaber duel on Starkiller Base is unforgettable. Ren is near-fatally wounded, but this scavenger from Jakku has never even wielded a lightsaber before, and still she keeps him at bay. At the darkest moment of the battle, she follows Maz's advice and lets the light guide her; she lashes out in defense, not rage. Rey is every child who's held a lightsaber toy in the backyard or playground and dreamed of saving the galaxy.

Rey goes on to complete the quest others couldn't: she finds Luke Skywalker on the remote planet of Ahch-To. *The Last Jedi* shows us he's not a willing teacher, and he traveled to an unfindable island for a reason. But Rey doesn't immediately get back into the *Millennium Falcon* and return to the Resistance. The determined spirit that helped her make it through years of solitude on Jakku takes over; she convinces Luke to train her in the ways of the Force by telling him, "I need someone to show me my place in all of this."

When Rey's power frightens Luke enough to halt their lessons, she doesn't turn to anger or sadness about being rejected. She continues training on her own. And, due to the machinations of Supreme Leader Snoke, she finds herself reconnected with a surprising person: Kylo Ren. They're taken aback by a Force connection, but over time, they find common ground. Rey turns

"Balance and energy. A force. . . . Inside me, that same force."

—Rey

to Kylo after her bewildering experience in the mirror cave on Ahch-To. Again, Rey maintains an open mind and is willing to put faith in Ben Solo—a man she saw murder his own father. She doesn't forget the horrific act, but she gradually senses his conflict and sees an opening to turn Ben back to the light, and she doesn't let go until he draws a line.

Kylo tells Rey that her parents were "filthy junk traders" who didn't want her. *The Last Jedi* director and writer Rian Johnson described it as the hardest possible thing she could have heard. Rey's been hinging a part of her identity on reconnecting with her family. She has to reassess who she is and do so among the turmoil of the Supremacy exploding around her. But she listens to the light side of the Force and commits to it, even after what she's heard about her parents, even after she no longer has a teacher to guide her. She brings hope where it is needed most: to Luke, Leia, and the Resistance.

Even beyond the trappings of the *Star Wars* saga—the First Order, the Resistance, the Force—Rey's story is inspiring, familiar, and timeless. Just because you come from nothing doesn't mean you're not part of the story. You're not no one, because anybody can save the galaxy. Anybody.

# Rose Tico

*"That's how we're gonna win. Not fighting what we hate; saving what we love."*

ᐳᓐᐱᐱ ᐁᕮᓇᐃ

Rose Tico is an everywoman, a working class member of the Resistance. She's proof that every single position counts. In a galaxy full of hotshot pilots, smugglers, nobles, and politicians, Rose is a mechanic and maintenance worker. She brings a fresh perspective on how war affects the average person; her idealistic nature and even her excitement is something we can identify with. As actress Kelly Marie Tran sees her, "Rose is not an amazing pilot or a Jedi, she's just strong in a different way, and I think that's how she holds her own."

In some ways, Rose is the personification of a fan in the *Star Wars* galaxy. She has a total fangirl reaction to Finn when she first meets him, stumbling over her words and calling him "The Finn." And when she presents an idea to General Leia Organa at the urging of her sister Paige in the comic *Forces of Destiny: Rose & Paige*, she admits to Paige, "Every time she talks to me I can barely function."

As Rose learns, meeting legends isn't always the experience one imagines. When she comes face-to-face with Finn in *The Last Jedi*, she expects him to be the First Order-turned-Resistance hero she's heard about. She has him on a pedestal. But then she realizes he's deserting, daring to run away when people like her sister Paige have sacrificed themselves to keep the spark alive. Rose shows how deep her integrity runs when she wipes away tears over losing Paige and

"Doing talking with Resistance
heroes is not my forte."

—Rose Tico

uses an electro-shock prod to knock Finn out, just like the others she's caught trying to escape the battle.

Rose isn't a leader when we first meet her, but she becomes a role model of sorts for Finn, showing him how to dedicate himself to the cause by example. And it's because of Finn that the character Rose, the fourth major new character in the sequel trilogy and the first Asian American female lead in *Star Wars*, was created. In early drafts, it was Poe who went with Finn on the side excursion to Canto Bight, but the team-up was boring. "It was just these two dudes on an adventure. I knew something was wrong when I looked at their dialogue and realized that I could interchange any of the lines," director Rian Johnson said in *The Art of Star Wars: The Last Jedi.* "There wasn't conflict between them. So I realized I had to come up with something else. Finn needing somebody else to go with who would actually challenge him and push him and contrast with him was where Rose came from." She's like the angel on Finn's shoulder.

Rose comes from a system ravaged by the First Order. She and Paige grew up on Hays Minor, a mining planet, longing to leave and travel the galaxy. And although they do eventually visit new planets with the Resistance, it's not quite in the tourist-seeing-the-sights experience Rose dreams of as a child. Because she's acquainted with the horrors the First Order brings to planets they want something from, Rose is motivated to help the Resistance from a place of empathy as well as determination. She isn't seeking revenge upon the First Order; she's committed to preventing them from doing further harm, to saving innocent lives.

Tran values Rose's humble background: "In a lot of movies today, we see people that are royalty, or are superheroes, or have magical powers . . . I love the idea of someone who might not necessarily be in the forefront of the action to begin with, someone who is like a cog in the machine that helps the Resistance keep going. But then at one point, you have to face your fears and have to be pulled into a situation and be able to face any challenge. It's such a huge deal to me, the idea that she's not necessarily special in the way that we have defined special before in other movies, or in other stories."

Even before she steps into the spotlight, Rose is doing more than just fixing things in the background. Her mechanical knowledge earns her the position of flight engineer aboard the *Cobalt Hammer*, the same bomber Paige is assigned to. Rose is inventive in her tinkering, perhaps more so because she hasn't received formal training. When General Organa asks her to come up with a technique to help bombers escape First Order detection in the novel *Cobalt Squadron*, Rose cobbles together a baffler, or a Resistance-cloak, "a poor but functional version of the real thing." It turns the bombers into stealthy ships, and in fact is so successful that the invention is later installed on the escape crafts evacuating from the *Raddus* to Crait in order to keep them hidden from the First Order.

Rose is supported and encouraged by her sister while she is alive, and driven forward still more powerfully after Paige's death. Rose cannot let her sister's sacrifice be in vain. The Mega Star Destroyer *Supremacy*'s ability to track the Resistance through hyperspace seems like an impossible problem, but Rose sees a solution. On her first ever Resistance mission without her sister, she disobeys orders and travels with Finn to Canto Bight, frees mistreated fathiers (Paige's favorite creature), and follows a risky plan intended to disable the First Order's tracker. Putting it all on the line for the sake of Paige and the Resistance, Rose becomes a hero.

Her heroism comes through in moments big and small. It comes through when she hands over her half of her pendant (an Otomok medallion shared with her sister) without hesitation because it's needed for the mission or when she leaves her Resistance ring with enslaved children on Canto Bight to give them hope. And it comes through when, as Finn tries to destroy the First Order's superlaser siege cannon on Crait by flying into it, in a "heroic" but likely futile death, Rose crashes into him and saves his life. She understands the real value not just of fighting what is evil, but in saving what is good.

"I wish I could put my fist through this whole lousy, beautiful town."

—Rose Tico

# Sabine Wren

*"Never get between a Mandalorian
and a weapons package."*

ᐯᔓᗐᓯᐯᐯ ᗡᔪᐯᓯᐯ

The word *Mandalorian* can often conjure the image of a certain kind of male warrior for *Star Wars* fans. But *Star Wars Rebels* redefines the idea of a typical Mandalorian by introducing Sabine Wren, a teenage one-time Imperial who defects to become a full-time rebel. The traditional armor she wears—five hundred years old, and carrying the history of battles and blood—has been reforged and colorfully repainted by Sabine to her liking. She adds her personal touch to everything, whether it's painting vignettes on the walls of her quarters aboard the *Ghost* or blowing up an Imperial base with panache. While the Empire is taking over Mandalore and blending the planet's martial warrior culture with Imperial authority, Sabine responds with defiance.

With freedom of expression at odds with the Empire's vision for the galaxy, Sabine uses her art to make a statement. She's the first character in the *Star Wars* galaxy to rebel through creative means by tagging Imperial outposts with the symbol of the phoenix (a symbol that later evolves into the Rebel Alliance starbird). She even repaints TIE fighters with garish hues, turning the bland gray and black Imperial equipment into personal works of art. Sabine also dyes her hair in bright colors and changes the designs on her armor to reflect special memories or recent events. She doesn't care if all of this makes her stick out as an Imperial target—it's too much fun to taunt the Empire.

"I want to believe we're doing good, making a difference . . . I need to know this isn't all for nothing."

—Sabine Wren

Her artistic pizzazz goes hand-in-hand with her demolitions expertise. Sabine learns about munitions at the Imperial Academy on Mandalore, and she later puts them to use in ways her instructors surely regret. She takes special pride in using explosives to destroy targets such as Imperial shipyards, but also in making the results beautiful. After one operation, she says, "Forget the explosion, look at the color."

Voice actress Tiya Sircar appreciates the character's creative and destructive sides. "She does it with flair, because she's also an artist. She's pretty rad, sassy, and strong. She's got this interesting sensibility about her. She's a teenager, and yet she's very sharp, she's very quick-witted, she's highly intelligent, and she's not worried about any of the superficial stuff that many teens are. She's really a fun character to play."

Sabine is a key part of the missions carried out by the Spectres aboard the *Ghost*. With her Mandalorian warrior training and education at the Imperial Academy, she's prepared to take on opponents in the air with a jetpack or hand to hand on the ground, and use her mechanical skills to activate or disable equipment. She can also understand multiple languages, once using her familiarity with Aqualish to help steal an Imperial shipment.

With her style and nature so upfront, Sabine can sometimes struggle to navigate the more subtle aspects key to insurrection. When the *Ghost* crew receives directives from an agent identified as Fulcrum, only Hera, the captain of the ship, has access to the full communication. It's hard for Sabine to understand that it's a secrecy born of necessity rather than a lack of trust. Sabine wants to know everything because she needs reassurance that they're actually getting somewhere with their actions against the Empire. She tells Hera, "I want to believe we're doing good, making a difference, but sometimes it seems like the harder we fight, the harder things get out there. I feel like we can't take down the Empire on our own."

As time goes by and the scattered Rebel groups unite into something more cohesive, Sabine grasps the bigger picture and takes on more responsibilities. Her Imperial past makes her the perfect operative to infiltrate the Empire's Skystrike Academy and extract students who want to defect to the Rebellion, including pilots we know from the original trilogy, Wedge Antilles and Hobbie Klivian.

When Sabine leaves Mandalore, it isn't entirely out of rebellion. She is also escaping a guilty chapter from her past. While at the Academy, she helps create a weapon known as the Arc Pulse Generator, which she later realizes could be used to enslave Mandalore to the Empire. She warns her family about the Empire's intentions, but her mother and clan leader Ursa Wren sides with the Imperials anyway. This conflict resurfaces after Sabine discovers the legendary Darksaber, a black-bladed lightsaber wielded by Mandalorian leaders for generations, in Darth Maul's hovel on Dathomir. Moved by what the Darksaber represents, she divulges this past shame to her friends on the *Ghost*, and embarks on the arduous task of banishing these demons when she trains to wield the Darksaber for the good of her people. Sircar especially liked seeing this different side of Sabine: "It was really wonderful, and so interesting, to get to see a character who is so guarded and so strong, and uses sarcasm and wit and snark at every opportunity, to be so vulnerable."

When Sabine returns home to try to recruit her family and other Mandalorians for the Rebellion, she is reunited with her mother. Sabine and Ursa aren't warm toward each other, but they come to an understanding, and Sabine remains on Mandalore for a while in an effort to make reparations for her mistakes. Having sabotaged the Arc Pulse Generator in its first incarnation, she's instrumental in destroying it a second time after the Empire has revived it, delivering it the fatal blow with the Darksaber. In the course of battle, she recognizes a leader in the former regent, Bo-Katan Kryze, and hands the Darksaber over to her before returning to the Rebellion.

In doing so she rejoins to the Spectres as a sort of family. Sabine, who once didn't trust in others, puts her faith in her teammates. Though Ezra seemingly gives his life to save Lothal, Sabine carries on. She tells the *Ghost* crew's story, and joins Ahsoka to search for the very much alive Ezra.

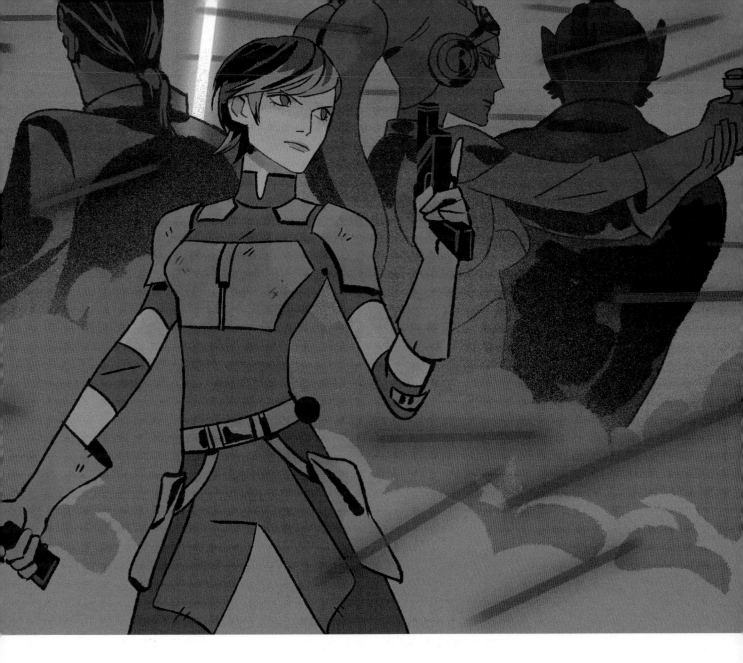

"We're a crew. A team. In some ways, a family."

—Sabine Wren

# Sana Starros

*"Move once, you won't be moving again."*

ᚾᚲᚾᚲ ᚾᛌᚲᛜᛜᚩᚾ

It's never too late to change your destiny. Introduced in the *Star Wars* comic, Sana Starros was born on Nar Shaddaa, known as Smuggler's Moon; for many years of her life, she lets her home direct her path and becomes a first-class smuggler, with skills to challenge Lando Calrissian or Han Solo. Her savviness means she considers every facet of a plan and finds ways to bury feints within feints, so that it's not always clear how many people she's crossing at the same time. Cutthroat and efficient, Sana gets the job done.

For one particular robbery, she and Han Solo even marry under pretense, but the scoundrel takes off with her cut. Sana's tendency to hold on to a grudge is clear when she tracks Han across the galaxy to make him pay (and when she later encounters her old flame, Chelli Aphra). When she finds him with Leia, she leans into greed and attempts to sell the princess to the Empire and collect a bounty. Sana looks down on Han's choice to help the Rebels. She tells Leia, "I haven't succumbed to the seductive wiles of the Rebellion."

But something about the Rebels gets under Sana's skin, and she sees a different course for her life. Ultimately, she uses her criminal tricks of the trade—cheating and bluffing—to the advantage of the Rebellion, and comes to realize, "Smugglers are only as good as the thing they're smuggling."

# Satine Kryze

*"War is intolerable. We have been deceived into thinking that we must be a part of it. I say the moment we committed to fighting, we already lost."*

ᚼᚲ ᚲᛁᚴᚹᛁ ᚴᛃᚢᚢᛁ

In a galaxy torn by war, the notion of pacifism can seem naively idealistic to some. But not to the Duchess of Mandalore, Satine Kryze. As Mandalore's latest civil war ends, she sees the culture's warrior past as the root of its problems, and she rebuilds the government upon the non-violent principles of the New Mandalorians. What follows are assassination attempts, another civil war, and the rise of a violent insurgent group called Death Watch (of which Satine's own sister Bo-Katan is a member). But Satine remains convinced throughout that these new rules are Mandalore's only hope for a future.

As we learn in *Star Wars: The Clone Wars*, Satine keeps Mandalore neutral in the conflict—despite her complicated past with the Jedi Obi-Wan Kenobi and her friendship with Senator Padmé Amidala. She leads her people through numerous hardships, such as the corruption of their Prime Minister and the influence of a dangerous black market, and she's able to do so in part because she raises an eyebrow at everything happening around her. When Obi-Wan tries to argue in favor of the Jedi's role in the Clone Wars, she observes archly, "The work of a peacekeeper is to make sure that conflict does not arise."

Anna Graves voiced Satine, "a spitfire lady with a lot of gumption. . . . I admire Satine's passion. She clearly cares for the people of Mandalore and their future. And the fact that she was brave enough to introduce new ideas of pacifism to a system whose history is based on being warriors shows she is willing to do anything to keep Mandalore safe from the Republic's growing power. I also love that she does not always hide her passion for Obi-Wan. He has been an important part of her past and she does not forget that . . . even when she tries to do so, she just can't forget."

# Seventh Sister Inquisitor

*"I only need you alive, that
doesn't mean in one piece."*

ᗺᑌᗰᎩᗰᑌᗷ ᗺᎨᑌᗷ ᐯᎨ ᗷᗅᑕᒪᎨᑌᗷᎨ

As a member of the Empire's Inquisitorius program, the Seventh Sister focuses on hunting down and eliminating the remaining Jedi in the galaxy who have survived the slaughter of Order 66. Caustic and capable, she's not to be trifled with, as we know from her first scene in *Star Wars Rebels*. Her zeal shows us what it's like to be an Imperial Force-user trying to climb to the top.

The Seventh Sister's vicious qualities make her a memorable villain. In service to the Sith Lord Darth Vader, she uses her dark side fueled Force abilities and ID9 seeker droids to ruthlessly toy with her targets; she's all about the cat-and-mouse game. She and fellow Inquisitor Fifth Brother kill nearly an entire ship's crew on a mission to abduct a Force-sensitive child. Just part of the job. And she relishes any opportunity to ignite her double-bladed, spinning lightsaber when the situation calls for action, which is anytime she encounters and torments Ezra Bridger and Kanan Jarrus.

# Shaak Ti

*"Don't let this be the end of the Jedi."*

⨝⧢⧢⌐ ↓1

The Jedi strike team on Geonosis in *Attack of the Clones* brings myriad lightsaber-wielding Force-users into the story, including Jedi Master Shaak Ti. A wise and patient member of the Jedi Council, the Togruta's story expands in *Star Wars: The Clone Wars* when she's appointed to supervise the production and training of the clone troopers on Kamino. In this role, she brings a measure of empathy toward the clones not generally shared by Kaminoans, treating them as the living beings they are instead of objects.

A devoted believer in the ways of the Jedi, Shaak Ti wants the Order to continue after the Jedi Purge. The night Anakin Skywalker becomes Darth Vader, she meditates and records a plea on a holocron. When Luke Skywalker finds the artifact years later, he hears Shaak Ti's message: "Don't let this be the end of the Jedi."

While portraying Shaak Ti, actress Orli Shoshan put her martial arts experience to the test. "My character required a lot of fight scenes," she says, "They liked how I used a lightsaber, and I didn't need a lot of extra training." However Shaak Ti's bulky costume made melee combat tricky: "Each time I was on set it took four hours to prepare my character. The entire costume was heavy, with a long tail, two horns, and a long skirt. It was hard to move! But I'm very happy that I had a chance to play this cool character. I'm proud to be a Jedi Master."

# Shmi Skywalker Lars

*"You can't stop the change any more than you can stop the suns from setting."*

ᔕᕼᗰ�I ᔕᛕYᗯᗩᒪᛕᕮᖇ ᒪᗩᖇᔕ

Shmi Skywalker, the mother of Anakin Skywalker, must say goodbye to her young son so he can fulfill his destiny and have a better life than she can provide. She gives him into the care of Jedi Master Qui-Gon Jinn, even though she knows she may never see him again, and in fact, it might be best for Anakin if she doesn't. As Anakin begins to leave, he returns to his mother and promises to come back to save her. She offers words of reassurance, but she also knows that he must be free to live his own life: "Be brave," she says. "Don't look back. Don't look back."

Shmi's life is one of hardship from the beginning. After her parents are captured by pirates, she is forced into slavery at a young age, first to Gardulla the Hutt, and then to the junk boss Watto. But she doesn't succumb to despair, and is able to maintain a courageous core optimism, instilling in her son values of compassion, kindness, and the necessity of helping others.

Portrayed by Swedish actress Pernilla August in *The Phantom Menace*, Shmi is strength personified. Her mettle isn't tested on the battlefield; instead, it's proven through her love for Anakin. August was nervous about playing Shmi because it was her first English-speaking role, but she did it anyway. August can relate to Shmi; she says, "It's a beautiful part; I love it very much. It's so warm. I feel very familiar about it because I have three kids myself. She's very brave, in a way, to let him go. She really does believe in him and that he's going to take responsibility for his life."

# Steela Gerrera

*"The time has come to take back our freedom."*

ꓵꓹ ꓦꓲꓦꓹꓘ ꓡꓦ77ꓦ17ꓘ

Steela doesn't want to be the leader of revolutionaries battling Separatist control on her homeworld of Onderon, but her mettle and courage make her a prime candidate. Voice actress Dawn-Lyen Gardner, who portrays the heroic character in *Star Wars: The Clone Wars*, identifies Steela's core in this way: "You totally get the sense that this girl can and will, literally, change her world."

Using guerrilla tactics she learns from Anakin Skywalker and Ahsoka Tano, Steela and her brother Saw execute targeted attacks against the Separatists with their compatriots. A skilled sharpshooter who prefers to let her weapon do the talking, Steela is unafraid in battle, and leads the Onderon resistance by example and with a drive to free her people. Steela wins that freedom for her home, but she pays the ultimate price. Her death inspires others, like her brother Saw, to continue the fight.

# Sugi

*"I know what I'm doing, and I will keep these people safe, my way."*

ᚅᚂᚔᚌ 1

*Honorable* is probably not the first word that comes to mind in the context of bounty hunters, but it should be when considering the mercenary known as Sugi. Hailing from the planet Iridonia, the Zabrak fighter doesn't take jobs for the sake of acquiring credits. She's not focused on glory or riches—in fact she'll cut her rate for the right cause. She only picks up work she believes in, because once she's committed, she's willing to put her life on the line.

Sugi's first appearance in *Star Wars: The Clone Wars* highlights her principled approach. Hired by Felucian farmers for protection, Sugi helps keep them safe from Hondo Ohnaka's pirate gang, and dismisses out of hand Hondo's attempt to buy her loyalty for double the money ("We don't break deals."). Her commitment to doing the right thing is noted by her peers, and by her niece, Jas Emari, whom Sugi encourages to escape Iridonia and become a bounty hunter. Jas follows in her footsteps, even flying Sugi's starship, the *Halo*.

# Sy Snootles

*"All in a night's work, baby."*

First seen as a singer in the Max Rebo Band at Jabba's palace in *Return of the Jedi*, Sy Snootles makes quite an impression with her weird vocal stylings and weirder appearance. The Pa'lowick performer's long limbs and cherry red lips stand out even in the crowd of quirky characters at Jabba's. The memorable crooner was first filmed as a puppet, brought to life by three operators manipulating rods and wires. Later, for the Special Edition release of the film, she was a digitally animated creation.

But Sy's more than she appears to be, and we later learn in *Star Wars: The Clone Wars* that her aspirations go beyond the stage. In her femme fatale past, Sy was once the paramour of Ziro, Jabba the Hutt's uncle. After he jilts her, she takes a job with Jabba to kill Ziro and steal his holodiary containing the Hutt Council records. Her last words to her former lover: "Next time you'll think twice about breaking someone's heart. Oh, wait, there won't be a next time."

# Tallie Lintra

*"Practice your dance moves later—we gotta fly."*

ↆꓘↇↇ1ⴸ ↇ1ⴷↆ7ꓘ

When the Resistance calls for reinforcements after the losses suffered during the attack on Starkiller Base, Rebel Lieutenant Tallissan "Tallie" Lintra is one of the starfighters who answers. Taking to space in *The Last Jedi*, Tallie joins the squadrons under Poe Dameron's command, launching into battle in a RZ-2 A-wing ahead of the Resistance bombers. She's capable in any sort of combat maneuver, whether she's on the offensive attacking a First Order Dreadnought or helping provide cover for the Resistance's retreat, and her skills impress Dameron. Her piloting abilities are a result of devoted training and the sort of use-whatever-resources-you-have attitude that puts her right at home in the Resistance. In Tallie's case, this means learning to fly in an RZ-1 A-wing used as a cropduster on her father's farm on Pippip 3. Fans can pilot her Resistance-issued fighter in the *Star Wars: Battlefront II* video game.

# Tam Ryvora

An inventive mechanic who longs for something more.

↓⊬ᒷ⎀ ⁊⎐⊬○⁊⊬ᴋ

What is a pilot without a mechanic? Tam Ryvora would have a snappy answer to that question. A key part of veteran pilot Jarek Yeager's garage in *Star Wars Resistance*, Tam works as a creative and determined technician, performing fix-it jobs for customers. But she wants more from life than just to be a mechanic in someone else's shop. In her downtime, Tam's restoring the *Fireball*, a broken-down ship she wants to eventually fly. Growing up with nothing, Tam wants to make a better life for herself. She dreams of wowing everyone on the Colossus with her spectacular piloting skills, and longs to join the Aces and live in Doza Tower, the luxurious building the racers call home.

Knowing the sting of being left behind by a friend seeking fame, Tam is guarded and skeptical of others, especially newcomers like cocky wannabe Ace, Kaz Xiono. She's formed a family of sorts with the garage crew and is reluctant to let anyone else in. Tam's had to learn how to rely on herself, so she's confident, knows exactly what she can offer, and isn't afraid to tell anyone who asks. Tam both impresses and infuriates Yeager with her inventive, sometimes crazy modifications on the ships they repair, all the while looking to the skies and longing to race.

# Tonnika Sisters

*"Survive until they won't let us."*

ᏔᎧᏁᏁᎥᏤ ᎒ᎥᏤᎥᏤ7Ꭻ

Con artists, thieves, and smugglers, sisters Brea and Senni Tonnika are more than capable of handling themselves in dangerous situations, and know the consequences otherwise: prison or death. With deception as one of their key talents, they survive by keeping on the move. You might remember the Kiffar siblings from the cantina scene in *A New Hope*. They're at the Mos Eisley bar hoping to get a lead on Han Solo and hand him over to Jabba the Hutt for a substantial reward—a reward they could use to buy escape and freedom.

Smart and resourceful, the sisters are driven by desperate choices in part because Brea is wanted for murder. But whether they are trying to steal royal jewels from House Organa or chase down a target, whatever the circumstances, the Tonnika sisters always have each other's backs.

# Torra Doza

A daring and competitive Ace pilot on the Colossus.

⅃� ⅂⎕⌀⅃⎕

The Aces, *Star Wars Resistance*'s daring pilots known for their flamboyant moves, are more than just racers; they're the protectors of the Colossus platform, a refueling station on Castilon, keeping the skies safe from pirates, the First Order, and other threats. At only 15-years-old, Torra Doza is the youngest—and one of the most daring—of these pilots. Torra lives for competition, and her racer has been customized for sprints. That her mother was once a pilot for the Rebellion helps fuel Torra's love of flying. She also wants to impress her father, Captain Doza, the owner of Colossus.

Torra takes daredevil risks in space, and her attitude translates to her style and decor. Her room is a bold purple and blue, and in it are enough toys derived from the galaxy to make any *Star Wars* fan jealous. It's here that she spends her downtime, relaxing and playing with her pet voorpak, Buggles. Torra doesn't have many pals, but she befriends the seemingly arrogant but actually awkward pilot Kaz Xiono. And though she's young, she's perceptive: she's one of the first to suspect Kaz's ties to the Resistance.

# Trios

*"We all do our duty."*

↓フ1◻⬃

As the third child of the king of the strategically valuable planet of Shu-Torun, Princess Trios doesn't expect to step directly into a leadership role. But Darth Vader has plans for her. In Marvel's 2015 *Darth Vader* comic, we see the Empire's push for increased production of ore from Shu-Torun causing friction, and inspiring an attempt on Vader's life. The Sith Lord's solution is to kill Trios's family and install her as queen of the Mid Rim world, as a vassal to the Empire. Following this horror, Trios must find a way to accept the new status quo. She has reserves of strength: she doesn't cower when she loses a hand to Vader's lightsaber. Trios looks to her future, and faces her new subjects with determination. What choice does she have?

Still, she proves herself loyal by claiming victory in a civil war, and later using her mining expertise to help oversee the Empire's extraction of kyber crystals from Jedha's ruins. But from the start, Trios isn't afraid of Vader. She's aware he's manipulating her on behalf of the Empire and finds ways to push back against his wishes, and remind him she's queen. She even channels his methods by putting naive royalty in place under her, telling the Sith: "I've found inexperienced youths not expecting power the most easy to manipulate, Lord Vader."

# Ursa Wren

*"Mandalore must rise by itself."*

ᒡᔨᓭ ᒡᔨᐱᐣ

When we first meet the Countess of Clan Wren, in *Star Wars Rebels*, she has a harsh and cold edge. Ursa Wren has been forced to make hard choices to protect her people. In the wake of her daughter Sabine's defection from the Imperial Academy on Mandalore, Ursa aligns Clan Wren with the Empire to safeguard their lives and honor. But this comes with a price; the gray armor the Wrens wear symbolizes the way the group has been ostracized by their own society. Given this, it's easy to understand Ursa not being thrilled about her daughter's return—in the company of Rebels, no less. Sabine's homecoming, and her effort to enlist the Wrens in the fight against the Empire, brings danger.

Ursa's resolute conviction makes her an unflappable ruler, but not a heartless one. When the Imperial Viceroy Gar Saxon tries to kill Sabine, Ursa stops him with a blaster bolt through the heart. She does so despite knowing the action means civil war. Her valor is as remarkable as her resolve. Ursa understands the consequences and knows it will be a struggle to find the right leader to take Mandalore into a new era, but she refuses help from the Rebellion: "The same Rebellion that sent you for my help? No, Mandalore must rise by itself."

# Val

A streetwise smuggler and saboteur who
knows how to read a situation.

Y⊠↲

*Proficient. Capable. Yearning. Present.* Actress Thandie Newton
uses these words to describe Val, her character in *Solo: A Star Wars
Story*. Tough, cool, and practiced with explosives, Val is the lieutenant of Tobias Beckett's criminal crew, and his paramour. But she
doesn't let her love for Beckett stop her from calling him out when
she thinks he's made a dumb move—like the decision to bring Han
Solo and Chewbacca into an important job when they only just met
them. Val is not here to tolerate anyone's nonsense. She's all about
getting the job done.

Newton credits the late producer Allison Shearmur for elevating
Val's role and presence in the film. "Alli Shearmur was the champion of my character, and her desire was to celebrate my ethnicity,
my hair texture, and to have me in my natural glory. She realized we
had an opportunity in this film to stake a claim that is of value in the
world." In fact, Val's hair and attire are inspired by political activist
Angela Davis and the Black Panther Party. Newton celebrated her
role in style during the 2018 Cannes Film Festival premiere of *Solo*,
wearing a custom Vivienne Westwood dress featuring a floral print
incorporating action figures of *Star Wars* characters portrayed by
black actors, such as Samuel L. Jackson's Mace Windu and Forest
Whitaker's Saw Gerrera.

"Our whole future depends on this one score and you bring in amateurs."

—Val

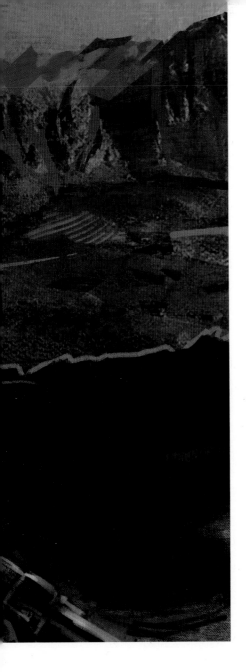

Val won't waste time putting on a sunny disposition to make others feel better. She's loyal to her team, yes, but also to herself, and that means she won't put on an act. She doesn't share personal details besides the fact that she was named after a valachord, a musical instrument, so it's not clear how her background may or may not inform her cynical attitude. But she doesn't need a reason to raise an eyebrow at new recruits.

Newton is clear on Val's value to the crew. "She's so calm. Nothing phases her. She's incredibly sure of herself. It's helpful when you're an expert in explosive devices and you have a number of them all over your body," she explains. "She knows how to protect herself and her team. She also knows how to manipulate an environment so they can work their way forward to their goals. She can manipulate huge areas of rock, huge pieces of landscape with these devices that she has. She's definitely someone you want on your side."

We get a sense of her athleticism during the conveyex heist on Vandor. Adventure-seeking tourists go to the planet to scale mountains and complete survival challenges, and it's the type of environment Val is prepared for. She's a climber, comfortable in precarious positions because she knows her limits and that she can ascend or rappel to get to just the right place. Without her agility and quick assessment of the situation—and her handmade explosives—the rest of the crew would likely not make it off the planet alive.

# Vi Moradi

*"Whoever you think I am, you're wrong."*

Y1 ᒐ◻7ᐊ╤1

Before heading to Disney Parks' *Star Wars*: Galaxy's Edge's Black Spire Outpost on Batuu for a new mission, Vi Moradi, the spy with the code name "Starling," worked for General Organa's Resistance to gather valuable information on the fearsome head of the Stormtrooper Corps, Captain Phasma. Her mission comes to the attention of one of Phasma's rivals within the First Order, Captain Cardinal, and it's his interrogation of her that provides the narrative structure of the novel *Phasma*. Author Delilah S. Dawson describes Vi as "like a female Poe Dameron: humor, ego, and talent, but with an added dash of James Bond. She's a spy with a long list of aliases and colored contact lenses, but she does admit to Cardinal that she only takes jobs that jibe with her heart and morals."

Vi's sure of herself, and knows how to best put her skills to use. She's able to turn her interrogation into a sort of high-stakes game, parceling out information to keep herself alive while also taking inventory of Cardinal's sympathies, interests, and weaknesses. Even when under strain, she pays attention to her surroundings and looks for useful information she might use to her advantage or share with the Resistance: no detail is too small. As she confides to Cardinal, "It's why I'm such a good spy."

# Zam Wesell

Mercenary assassin who can change
her appearance at will.

ᐰᏦ᠘ ᗡᐺᐺᐺᐺᐺ ᠘ᐺᖷ

Appropriately for a shape-shifting character, the development of Zam Wesell went through a number of forms before her appearance in *Attack of the Clones*. The bounty hunter was first conceived as a human male, then a human female, then an alien, and in her final form as a female Clawdite changeling, thanks to George Lucas. "I thought Zam needed to be more exotic and interesting," he said, "and this was a way to do that."

As an assassin, Zam possesses the skills you'd associate with the notorious gig. She's good at hitting targets from a distance, making speedy getaways, and knowing where to source the right equipment for her jobs. And it's intriguing that despite the fact that she can choose to look like any humanoid, she takes on the appearance of a woman. We encounter her in the film when she attempts to kill Padmé Amidala on the orders of her associate, Jango Fett, first by bombing the senator's ship, later by releasing poisonous creatures via droid into her living quarters. When

Obi-Wan Kenobi and Anakin Skywalker uncover her plot, Zam doesn't panic, fleeing the scene and steering an airspeeder through Coruscant's busy traffic with professional cool.

It's no wonder she's so calm. Born on the harsh-climated planet of Zolan, Zam devotes herself to learning from ancient warrior-knights known as the Mabari. Zam's a Clawdite who knows what she wants, and she decides her goal is wealth. She puts her hard-won talents on the table for profit.

Zam's appearance switches between human and alien in her scenes. Industrial Light & Magic was responsible for the digital transition to Clawdite, but actress Leeanna Walsman brought Zam's human form to life. Getting into Zam's costume, which included forty-five pieces of armor, helped Walsman inhabit the bounty hunter. "The costume and the weaponry really help make the character," she says. "You look at yourself in the mirror and you say, 'This is how I'm going to be.'"

# About the Artists

**Alice X. Zhang** is a Chinese-American illustrator with an enduring interest in cinema, comics, and pop culture. She holds a BFA from the Rhode Island School of Design, and her clients include BBC Worldwide (*Doctor Who, Sherlock*), Marvel Studios, DC Films, and Lucasfilm. [pp. 12, 86, 159, 186-187, 224-225]

**Amy Beth Christenson** has been working for Lucasfilm companies as a concept artist for eighteen years. She is the art director for *Star Wars Resistance* and has worked on *Star Wars* projects throughout her career, including *Star Wars Rebels, Star Wars: The Clone Wars*, and *Star Wars: The Force Unleashed*. [pp. 37, 212, 216]

**Annie Stoll** is a New York-based, Grammy-nominated art director and an award-winning designer and illustrator. A lifelong Star Wars fan, she has worked with Lucasfilm on a number of projects, including Sabine: *My Rebel Sketchbook* with author Dan Wallace. She is also the co-curator of the people-positive anthology *1001 Knights*. Annie currently works at Sony Music where her recent clients include Columbia, Legacy, and RCA, for artists such as Pentatonix and Weird Al Yankovic. [pp. 60, 68-69, 104-105, 130, 162-163, 190-191, 200]

**Annie Wu** is an American illustrator currently based in Chicago. She is the creator of the upcoming Image Comics series *Dead Guy Fan Club*, a neo-noir black comedy. [pp. 64-65, 81, 101, 119, 156, 178-179, 184-185, 199]

**Christina Chung** is a Taiwanese-Hong Konger-American illustrator currently based in Brooklyn. She holds a BFA in Communication Design from the Pratt Institute. Through a line and pattern-based style, she creates illustrations that are intricate, narrative and infused with symbolism. Her clients include *The New York Times*, Amazon Publishing, Cathay Pacific, NPR, and *Scientific American*. [pp. 31, 53, 78-79, 120, 145, 176, 220]

**Cryssy Cheung** is a New York-based art director, award-winning designer, and multi-disciplinary illustrator known for comic book covers, editorial illustration, and licensed *Star Wars* art. She holds a BFA in Computer Art, Computer Animation and Visual Effects from New York's School of Visual Arts. Her clients include Eater, Moleskine, Adobe, CBS, Marvel, Valiant, IDW, EasyJet, and DC Comics/Vertigo. [pp. 18, 32, 45, 124, 138, 155, 172, 207]

**Eli Baumgartner** is a Vienna-based freelance illustrator focusing on 2D, sequential, and illustrative art. Having worked as a concept artist and cinematic lead for an indie platformer game at Roaring Fangs, Eli also illustrates covers and comics for clients, and is co-creator of the webcomic *Heart of Gold*, together with Viv Tanner. [pp. 56, 82, 141, 142, 152-153, 223]

**Elsa Charretier** is a French illustrator and comic book artist. After debuting on *C.O.W.L.* at Image Comics, Elsa co-created *The Infinite Loop* with writer Pierrick Colinet at IDW. She has since worked at DC Comics (*Starfire, Bombshells, Harley Quinn*), Marvel Comics (*The Unstoppable Wasp*) and Random House (*Windhaven*, written by George R.R. Martin). She has written *The Infinite Loop* vol.2 as well as *Superfreaks*, and is a regular artist on the *Star Wars Adventures* book series. [pp. 41, 62, 70, 92-93, 112-113, 175, 208]

**Geneva Bowers** is a self-taught, North Carolina-based illustrator who enjoys working with color and adding whimsy with a touch of realism and happiness. Her clients include *ImagineFX, Advanced Photoshop, Photoshop Creative, FIYAH*, Stranger Comics, and Penguin Random House Children's Books. [pp. 26, 54, 102, 127, 148-149, 180-181, 226]

**Jen Bartel** is an illustrator and comic artist who specializes in drawing strong ladies. She is best known for her ongoing cover work for clients like Marvel, DC/Vertigo, and Dark Horse. She is the artist of the upcoming Image Comics book, *Blackbird*. [front and back covers, pp. 8, 110]

**Jennifer Aberin Johnson** is a Toronto-based game developer, comic artist, and illustrator. She is fascinated with portraying otherworldly landscapes and strives to promote diverse voices in speculative fiction. [pp. 17, 49, 76-77, 94, 114-115, 132, 151, 195]

**Jenny Parks** is a Colorado-based freelance illustrator and nerd with a degree in scientific illustration and a love for drawing animals. While she generally specializes in painting cats dressed as pop-culture characters, she'll draw any manner of creature, real or imagined. She is the author and illustrator of *Star Trek Cats* and *Star Trek Cats: The Next Generation*. [pp. 98]

**Karen Hallion** holds a BFA in illustration from the Ringling School of Art and Design. Based in Massachusetts, she has done licensed work for Her Universe, Hank Green/DFTBA Games, Patrick Rothfuss, Marvel, Lucasfilm, Cartoon Network, DreamWorks, Cryptozoic Entertainment, Topps, Disney, and Disney Imagineering. She was a featured artist at the 2015 and 2016 *Star Wars* Celebration Art Shows, and a 2017 guest at VidCon, NerdCon, and Awesome Con. [pp. 46, 90-91, 116-117, 146, 171, 183, 211, 219]

**Little Corvus** is an Eisner-nominated queer non-binary Latinx comic artist and illustrator based in Seattle. A graduate of the School of Visual Arts with a BFA in Cartooning, Little Corvus' work has been featured both online and in print anthologies. They love positive, diverse stories, and the color pink. [pp. 24-25, 38, 74, 97, 136-137, 161, 228]

**Sara Alfageeh** is a Jordanian-American illustrator passionate about nuances in visual storytelling, teaching, and culturally diverse representation in media. She focuses on the spaces where art and identity intersect. She works primarily with digital mediums, but also knows the true satisfaction that can come from bold pen lines and fresh ink. [pp. 14-15, 59, 85, 135, 168-169, 188, 204]

**Sara Kipin** is a Burbank, California-based illustrator and visual developer who holds a BA from the Maryland Institute of Art. She has done TV animation work for Marvel, Moving Colour, and Cartoon Network, and illustrations for Cosmopolitan and Leigh Bardugo's *New York Times* bestselling novel *Language of Thorns*. [pp. 22, 34-35, 67, 89, 128, 192-193]

**Sarah Wilkinson** travels the world with her art studio, Studio de Sade, bringing her art to conventions and art shows. She has worked in the comic book and trading card industries for more than a decade, with clients that include Topps, IDW, and Lucasfilm, and her art has also been used for book covers and interior illustrations, toy designs, and more. [pp. 21, 42, 50, 73, 109, 166-167, 203]

**Viv Tanner** is a Vienna-based illustrator who holds a degree in 2D Animation from the Lucerne School of Applied Sciences and Art, and focuses on freelance Illustrations for magazines, comics, and books. Together with Eli Baumgartner, Viv is the creator of the webcomic *Heart of Gold*. [pp. 28-29, 107, 123, 164, 196, 215]

# Acknowledgments

To my sister Nicole and to my friends Andrea, Sarah, Jenn, Christy, Christine, and Lisa, for being incredible sources of inspiration and always having my back.

To my editor Steve Mockus, for giving me a chance, answering many questions, and providing immeasurable help. To Julia Patrick, for thoughtful insights. To Michael Morris and Jenna Huerta for their beautiful design work, and to Lia Brown, Victoria Chao, Steve Kim, and Michelle Clair, for helping keep things on the rails. To Caitlin Kennedy, for being a champion. To everyone at Lucasfilm and Chronicle who helped make this book happen.

To all the talented and fierce artists who contributed their stunning art to this book.

To the galaxy far, far away, for being a fictional universe that gives me a lift whenever I need it.

And finally to Aaron, for endless support and patience.